Here Comes the Roar

Previous Winner of the Katherine Anne Porter Prize
in Short Fiction
Barbara Rodman, series editor

The Stuntman's Daughter by Alice Blanchard
Rick DeMarinis, Judge

Here Comes the Roar

by Dave Shaw

2003 WINNER, KATHERINE ANNE PORTER PRIZE IN SHORT FICTION
Marly Swick, Judge

University of North Texas Press
Denton, Texas

10 9 8 7 6 5 4 3 2 1

Permissions:
University of North Texas Press
P.O. Box 311336
Denton, TX 76203-1336

The paper used in this book meets the minimum requirements of the American National Standard for Permanence of Paper for Printed Library Materials, z39.48.1984. Binding materials have been chosen for durability.

Library of Congress Cataloging-in-Publication Data

Shaw, Dave, 1966–
    Here comes the roar / by Dave Shaw.
        p. cm.
    "2003 Winner, Katherine Anne Porter Prize in Short Fiction."
    ISBN 1-57441-170-5 (pbk. : alk. paper)
    1. Psychological fiction, American. 2. Separation
(Psychology)—Fiction. 3. Loss (Psychology)—Fiction. I. Title.
    PS3619.H35745 H47   2003
    813'.54—dc21
                                                    2003012961

Here Comes the Roar is the 2003 winner of the Katherine Anne Porter Prize in Short Fiction

This is a work of fiction. Any resemblance to actual events or establishments or to persons living or dead is unintentional.

The photograph on the cover, "Careers," is by Will Connell and is reproduced with permission of the Will Connell Collection, UCR/California Museum of Photography, University of California, Riverside.

Text design by Carol Sawyer of Rose Design

For my wife, daughter, son, parents, and sister,
other family near and far, and friends old and new.

*C*ontents

Acknowledgments

The author would like to express his sincere gratitude to author Lee Zacharias and the other exceptional faculty at The University of North Carolina at Greensboro's M.F.A. Program in Fiction Writing for their advice and encouragement throughout the crafting of these stories, as well as to the North Carolina Arts Council for a Writer's Fellowship that enabled the composition of "Diving with the Devil" and the editing of all of the fiction contained here.

The author also gratefully acknowledges the editors of the following publications for their time and expertise, and for originally publishing this work: *Literal Latte,* for "Any Myth You Can Imagine," which appeared in the May/June 1998 issue as "The Unexplained"; *Carolina Quarterly* (Fall 1997) and *Southern Exposure* (Spring 1998), for "Holding Pattern at D. C. National"; England's *Stand Magazine* (Fall 1998), for "The Lover, the Diver, the Professor, the Pilot," the story upon which "Diving with the Devil" is based; and *Greensboro Review* (Summer 2000), for "A Cure for Gravity."

*A*ny Myth *You Can Imagine*

I cannot escape him. At night he rides the Flying Horses. Daringly he clutches the mane of a steel-eyed mare, charging his ebony horse to a whimsy of carnival music, leading a wild, circular stampede. Carousel bulbs sparkle and blink in a rapids full of light. He and the children stretch, elongate, will themselves to reach silver rings off the chute as their horses whip past. Two rings, four, leaning farther, six at a time, nearly thrown from their rides, as many rings as they can grab before the carousel swings them away into the dark. They take chances, loosen grips, fight common sense and centrifugal force. They hope for the winner, the gold ring, a free ride. His tie loose as a kite tail, he grins like the nine-year-olds flying along with him—a big kid himself, the embodiment of innocence—as if he were not playing only for sympathetic hearts. The carousel swings him round again, back out into the lights, and he waves the golden ring. He soars. He laughs, as if he has won something from me. He has. He is the man who has stolen my wife.

Music quiets. Children shout disappointment. The horses have fallen to a slow trot. Lights flicker white to red, and back to white. My boy Eliot pulls at my watch and loosens me from my daze. "Now, Dad," he shouts. I lift him up and away onto a passing pony. He waves his ticket and kicks to spur along his wooden horse. The ancient ride smells of gunpowder and sawdust. The man who has stolen my wife has dismounted to hand his gold ring to a tow-headed boy, Tom Lockhart's youngest son, who quickly jumps onto the platform and struggles up onto his mount. The man finds Tom Lockhart's wife, sitting in a short skirt on a skee-ball lane, showing more leg than she wants. And what's become of Tom Lockhart? It is a perpetual motion machine. The music starts again.

The man who stole my wife is everywhere. For sanctuary I sit in my own quiet, my lunch hour each day in the old Glass Museum in Sandwich. But he enters and pretends to read placards and to study blown glass, and winks at two college girls off the beach dawdling in pink bathing suits. After work, on board the ferry home, the docks at Woods Hole fade into dull fog and he leans against a deck railing, smoking, smiling at an old maid struggling up metal steps. Gulls trailing our ship dive to eat off the wake. On the island, at a red light in Oak Bluff, he strums his coupe's engine, and to the desired effect: turned heads, a friendly grin, perhaps even a wink returned. At the overlook in Aquinnah, I find him snapping pictures like a tourist, though he is only an islander lying in wait for conversant divorcées and surely is disinterested in yellow cliffs and ocean views. He lingers only to mention the roaring romance of the waves or the deep angle of the drop or some such words too sentimental to repeat here. It has only been two weeks since he stole my wife. I find him everywhere.

I do not believe in mysticism, God, the soul, or even UFOs. Aside from physics, I believe in no universal connection between man, nature, and sky. Yet I cannot dismiss this phenomenon, this presence each place I venture, and my inability to remove him from my mind. For he is both a man and much more than a man; he is many men. He is a blue suit, a fisherman, a diver, or an over-sexed adventurer lazing in for the summer. He is Asian, Latino, white, or black. He wears caps, goes hatless, has a grey head, or jet hair. He stands in crooked posture with his hands in his pockets, demure in his carriage. He strides with purpose through shop doorways, a brazen piece of sidewalk traffic, a real cowboy. He is a wisp. He is an anchor, a three-day growth and the smell of tobacco, a heartbeat you hear as he passes.

He is different each time I encounter him, and of course he is the same. He always reminds me of Rachel, as he is supposed to, simply that she has left me for him. His eyes, too, are the same each time I find him: cracks, slits of light under a closed door that hides the treachery of a room inside which you never may enter. I cannot escape him.

My only solace is night sky, a land breeze and the sound of surf up through a patch of pines, wet grass like meadow grass on bare feet, and two open windows of light hanging in our other-wise dark house up the hill, as if the windows were open holes in the night itself. But I am no romantic. I aim my telescope at galaxies and the machinations of gravity, the dirty atmosphere—smog and dust twinkling the stars—and the red planet, a dead planet, rising inland west. All of it is simple. All of it is science. And where is the moon? Not to rise for another hour. Ptolemy, Copernicus, Newton, Einstein, every paradigm falls to cracks over decades and centuries. Two weeks is no time, out here with night sky and the smell of spruces. In a year, life with Rachel will be as obsolete as a model of flat Earth.

"Dad?"

My boy Eliot has startled me again, this voice in the darkness. "You're getting good," I say, "slinking up on me like that. You'd make a fine Navy SEAL."

"Dad?" he asks, and I know the question is coming, one of these times, the one question he has not yet asked, but must, because he is only a boy who wants to know when his mother will return. And how shall I answer him?

"Dad, can we see Saturn?"

"Of course," I cry, and I swing the scope around, quickly finding reference on zenith and azimuth. Stars smear to comets in the scope. I sight the planet and focus, and there—the thin ring he loves.

He looks through the scope and I know he is smiling. "Saturn really goes on forever," he says, waving a miniature hand. "I mean Saturn just keeps on going. I can see the rings spinning."

"Not really," I tell him. "You only think you can see it."

"No," he says. "You could see it, too, if you really wanted to."

My boy is quite the philosopher.

"Which is older?" I ask him. "God or Saturn?"

"God," he says.

"Saturn," I say. The breeze raises the hairs on my legs. "Saturn is billions of years old. Man only a couple hundred thousand, and man created God because he needed Him."

"I don't get it," he says.

"Man needed God, so he dreamed Him up," I say. I can tease him this way only because he is utterly unshakable in his faith— her doing. And because I must want him to show me this piece of her now.

"Dad?" my boy asks. He steps away from the telescope. He crosses his arms, then uncrosses them and leaves them dangling at his sides.

"Yes?"

"Dad—?" But he does not finish the question, so I do not try to answer.

Another two weeks, and still the wife-stealer is everywhere: strolling in his tan down the hot sand along Vineyard Sound, tossing horseshoes in a shaded church lawn in Chilmark, hoisting a mainsail in a shallow cove, fighting the wind with a chiseled look out at Cape Pogue as if he possesses a superior life over on Nantucket. He stations himself to be seen, though not by me, but by housewives in crisis or someone's cousin in for a weekend or women far too young for him.

If the key to understanding quirks of the psyche is awareness, then I should be free of him. Because, yes, his presence has forced me to remember the details. Rachel and I walking through our house, teacups in hand, the wood floors creaking and wind off the ocean whistling in through the porch railings. Rachel and I in our own separate daydreams. We pass without speaking, lost in our private spheres, something new for the two of us: both of us trapped in our own thoughts instead of only me. I never noticed she had begun to wear make-up again, to spend more time combing out her bay hair, to put it in braids. I never paused to study the sway of her hips as she walked away from me, humming to herself, watering bluebells in niched windows which suddenly were flourishing. I never knew the sundresses were newly bought. I did not study the brightness under her lashes or the smile in the lines easing from her eyes. I never wondered why she swept on days the maid did not come. When the afternoon thunderstorms brought rattling plates and fragility to our house, she never blew me a kiss, and I never wanted one. The windows were always open and the house always carried that chill—but a comfortable one, I thought—that vigorous breeze of ocean air and a taste of wet sand, the hope of summer. I knew nothing.

Now, despite the distance of a few weeks, I must confess that I still am a bit thrown to be left with only a quickly inked note, a curt apology with no description of *him*. Where did she meet him? At a fund-raiser for her Organization for the Preservation of Island History? At the Bingo Club and its rooms full to the rafters each Wednesday night with people sweating, feeling their new luck? And what about our son? It is easy to explain lover leaving lover, wife leaving husband in this case, but how does a mother leave a son? Perhaps by her design he is to be another reminder for me that she is gone, a complement to my visions of those narrowed eyes who stole her away.

"Dad, can we go to Flying Horses?"

The sun sets on the water, a glare in through the pines. My boy and I are sitting on rocking chairs out on the old porch. The air, calm, holds a sour edge of dead fish.

"Should we go to Flying Horses," I ask, "or look through the telescope tonight? There's a partial lunar eclipse in an hour."

"Which one is a lunar?" my boy asks, swinging his feet, which cannot reach the floorboards.

"It's the one where the Earth casts its shadow on the moon. Besides," I say, smacking at a horsefly, "it's very hard to have a solar eclipse after dark."

"Oh, yeah," he says.

"Oh, yeah," I kid him.

"We should go to Flying Horses," he says.

The least he deserves is Flying Horses. "You have very messy hair," I tell him. "We'll have to wash it, I suppose."

The last sliver of sun sinks, reddens a cloud off the water.

"It's still possible," my boy says.

"Fixing that hair of yours?"

"No," he says, giggling. "A solar eclipse. I mean, in the dark."

"And how is that possible?"

"Anything's possible," he tells me.

These, of course, are her words. For a minute we both rock quietly, enjoying her presence.

The trips each night to Flying Horses, watching the dance between Tom Lockhart's wife and one version of the man who stole mine, only remind me of the old cliché often spoken by man to man—never woman to woman—in order to invalidate pain. It involves immediately climbing back into the saddle. This trite saying becomes the backbone of my personal pep talks after—all told—a month and three weeks of empty clothes hangers jingling in the drafts in our closets, after two dreams about tornadoes bringing the beach to our back door, and, of course, after many more encounters with the man who stole Rachel.

He walks his collie on the piers, squinting—he only squints—at the fishermen's wives; wearing riding gear and a contented smile he grooms a saddle horse at the stables; on clay courts nestled between firs, I find him playing tennis with a soon-to-be widow. Each day I drive through flesh-colored dunes with their tufts of grass always bending in the breeze; there is ridiculous optimism in the clouds and a soothing wind in my ear. But there is always a viper within my glance, a stranger waiting to step from shadow into my horizon. Rachel never is with him.

I would settle for a glimpse of her, even if she were with him.

A saddle, of sorts: a gathering in Vineyard Haven at Robin Everson's house, a tie and jacket affair with plenty of drinks to start "precisely at sunset." In an earlier era it might have been called a cocktail party. I arrive alone, having left Eliot with the bourbon-stealing college girl whom Rachel and I always use each summer. Given the legendary tales about other sitters which are part of our island lore, it is a common assumption she is the best available. Twice after nights out, Rachel and I have found her sleeping in her underwear on the couch.

The Eversons' house is tremendous, a cape, of course, a three-story remnant of old money. In daylight the siding shows tear streaks, scars of unforgiving weather; in waning light their home is a fortress. I park in the street, walk up through the coarse-bladed grass that grows so easily in ocean air. To cut the dusk, Everson's wife has lit lanterns which trace up to the house a drive-way black as running ink. In the open windows, silhouettes glide together and separate again. Word spreads here on the island. Surely, they are talking about me now, will talk in trios while I am inside when my attentions are elsewhere, will talk after I leave, openly and boisterously if enough has been drunk. I have done it myself, reveling in others' broken lives, seeing them only as enter-tainment. On the front step, already I hear their murmurings. It is nobody's fault there is nothing else really to talk about.

Everson's wife ushers me in. She is a dainty, top-heavy thing in high heels. Her hair has been dyed brown for twenty years of denial and regrets about not starring at the Hollis Street Theatre. The rumor says she makes herself a short Demerol cocktail with every meal. "Hello, Margaret," I say. "You look wonderful."

"So good to see you out, Evan," she replies. "It's as if you've gone into hiding. So understandable really. But, oh, my, perhaps I shouldn't have . . ."

"Really, Margaret. You know me better than that. I'm fine, really."

"It's just that when a man's wife . . ."

"No need to rehash, Margaret. We know what happened."

In the living room she leaves me suspended in the after-air of her perfume, alone amidst the usual crowd, conversing, glasses in hand, on cozy boccara islands. Already I wear around my neck a sign screaming "Cuckold." For a few moments, we all make use of the corners of our eyes. It is old Everson to the rescue. He hands me a gin. Light from a hanging lamp shines on his forehead as if it is a thought showing itself. It was true that many years ago his daughter had eloped with a greasy painter from Provincetown and that Everson now often gambled the dailies at Aqueduct. With his short, jagged beard and small ears he is the prototypical old goat.

"How's the slice?" I finally ask, and take a long, warm sip of the gin.

He smiles great relief. I have steered us safely, for the moment, to talk of male ritual, equally important in a way as the unmentionable. "Well, in fact I've fixed the old slice," he says. I can tell by his grin he has a quip coming.

"It's about time," I grin back.

"Yes," he says, "it really was quite an accomplishment. I've converted it into a terrific hook."

We both laugh a little, too much for so mild a joke. The rest of the room dropped to whispers until our laughter, and now the other conversations resume their volume, secure that I will not be a sap ruining their party. Everson fades back into the herd, free to worry to his guests about homosexuality or the Harbor Management Committee. In the murmur I find cover, and resolve to leave as soon as it is not entirely obvious. I search for my own island of conversation away from happily married men and happily divorced men who can joke easily about golf or fishing. The house smells of roses, although the vases are empty. Rachel is nowhere in the crowd. I had not expected her to embarrass me by bringing her new man, or even by coming alone, but the place seems occupied, quite suddenly, with only cardboard cut-outs of people in pose.

The old house is full of knaves and alcoves, and finally I find Tom Lockhart's wife drinking alone, standing in the protection of a jutting brick wall and two large ferns as if she has been positioned by interior decorators. She wears a dark green evening dress cut very low in the front, with a strategically placed rose-colored brooch.

"Hello, Elizabeth," I say. The two of us safely are cut-off from the pack. She has gone braless again.

"Evan," she says, tilting her head. Her hazel eyes already have begun to glaze. Many years ago, when her eldest son was failing out of a very private secondary school, we flirted quite openly and even once managed to find a quiet porch at another party to kiss. She is only a few years older than I. She was a dangerous kisser, pushing down a strapless to expose her breasts, wanting to feel the cold night against her skin, asking me to lower my lips when anyone could have walked out to find us. She was the one to say a week later, once her son had cheated and prayed his way through another quarter, that neither of us wanted anything more to come of it.

"Where's Tom?"

"Edinburgh," she says, "for the summer. IVC is branching to the UK and he's what they call their man on the point. They make it sound like a war. You take point. I'll take the rear, blah blah blah with these men. What is it you do again? I know you've told me a million times, but it always escapes me."

I tell her again about the tedium of the programs up at Digital. "My damn feet are killing me," she says. She bends over to unhook her heels. Her dress gathers to show the fall of her breasts. She reminds me only of the general urges I nearly have forgotten about, and I have no real desire to go to bed with her. She kicks her heels disgustedly into a corner. "I hate these damn things," she says. "Can I have your drink?"

She takes my gin, wobbling, standing now three inches shorter, and suddenly vulnerable.

"That's better," she says, stepping toward me. The liquor has opened her pores and surrounded her in fumes. "Did you get a good look?"

"At what?"

"When I bent over for you just now. Did you get a good look?" she smiles.

"It was a marvelous look."

"I thought you were ignoring me."

"How could I ignore you, Elizabeth?"

"All those nights at that flying merry-go-round," she says. "You never speak to me."

"I'm a little preoccupied," I say. "Besides, you have a new friend, I've noticed."

She stares, as much as she can stare drunk as she is, deciding, I know, whether to show me a playful cattiness or anger. She suddenly begins fumbling for her heels without looking down for them, holding her dress to her chest as she gropes. "What are you insinuating?" she asks.

"Nothing, Elizabeth. I've noticed him, is all."

"I don't know what you're talking about," she says, finally managing to slide one heel on, then giving in and letting the dress fall from her chest again to find the other.

"I understand," I say. "Look, if anyone should understand—"

"You think that since Tom is away I'm out breaking in couches."

"Elizabeth, I only—"

"Well, that's not how it is. Tom and I are great, Evan. I can't help it if everyone's life isn't in the same disarray that yours is."

The whole island knows this is untrue, that the Lockharts' marriage has come and gone except for signatures on papers.

"Is that why you came over to talk to me?" she says. "To get a little something since the wife left?"

Her defensiveness angers me more than it should. True, I am miffed that she will not agree to see our marriages on equal ground, and that her attempts to flirt with me have been turned to become my own imagination. Perhaps it is the sudden, inexplicable nature of her rage which angers me. Perhaps she has visions like I do. Perhaps she sees her husband looking foolishly into sea and space wherever she ventures, whenever she is not with him, whenever she is with her new man.

"Listen, Rachel—" I say.

"Oh, that's a bad one," she snaps. "Mixing up the names. Here's a tip. Always try to keep the names straight. You'll have much better luck getting a piece, Tom."

"I'm Evan."

She stomps away. Her dress drags leaves off the giant ferns. One of her heels snaps on the hardwood. Her steps echo a broken gallop.

A minute or two later, Everson's wife sees me off at the front door. "I'm having a mix-and-match party for new and old singles," she says to me gleefully. "Will you come, Evan?"

"I'm still married, Margaret." But I allow the thought to provide only momentary comfort as I step into the night.

I take the long route home to East Chop, the road along Vineyard Sound, past the pond, now dark, a hollow in the night. At least a week or two each winter it used to freeze for Rachel and Eliot to skate. I wind across the cliffs at Aquinnah, through ocean mist and gin mist and stars. I drive through apparitions of Kerri, the sitter, waiting for me at the house, and the nights taking her home after Rachel and I had been out being entertaining at parties.

The gropings. Kerri's hand on my knee as I shifted gears up the hill to her parents' summer home, only a mile drive, taking my foot off the gas, her hand on my thigh, then fidgeting with my zipper. "Do not," I would say, though not always right away. She giggled, open came my fly. Her breath warmed my neck. Her breasts warmed my arm. "Do not," her hand in my trousers, and then, finally, every time, I would stop her before she brought me past that point I considered to be the marker of faithfulness. Every time except one night after Rachel and I had spent several hours drinking out on a sailboat with the Thompsons.

At home, I find Kerri feigning sleep on a living room couch, wearing only a black bra and panties, arching her back slightly for effect in the harsh tv light. Her sandals, the always unbuttoned blouse, the short black skirt lay on the floor. "How is this supposed to make me feel?" I said to Rachel when we had found her this way before. "This young woman sleeping half-nude in our house?"

"She's a girl," Rachel said. "Put your brain back in and drive her home."

An old Billie Holiday c.d. plays lightly in the background, one of Rachel's favorites. The music is lilting and synchronized to Kerri's exaggerated breathing.

"Put your clothes on," I say. "It's time to go home."

"I'm sleepwalking," she says, smiling, rising from the couch with her eyes still closed. She becomes a silhouette in front of the tv.

"My son had better be asleep, with you in your underwear like this."

"Of course," she says, stepping slowly toward me, still with her eyes shut. It has been years since I was with someone in her early twenties, fourteen or fifteen years at least. The sweep of her hair around her shoulders, the tautness in her chest, the tension in her thighs—I tell her again to put on her clothes. She opens her eyes, dark in the tv light, then flickering.

"There's no reason for us not to anymore," she says, shifting the cant of her hips.

"Kerri—," and the music silences between cuts. I let her loosen my tie. The saddle, I remember, as if the saddle is indeed a solution. It is. She stands on her tiptoes to kiss me. I let her. Her lips are hot. She tastes like smoke. Her elbows jut to unhook the clasp behind her back, and the bra falls to the floor. She steps out of her panties, betrays no tan lines. The music starts again.

Afterward, unclothed in a pallor of light and static from the tv, we lie side by side, without touching, on a cold rug. She thanks me and says to keep her bra. Our age difference crumples me.

"Call me," she says, and then adds, for the first time, my first name.

"Do you want a ride?"

"No need for that anymore," she says, smiling. "It's only a mile, Evan."

I glare at her as if she is the reason Rachel left me.

Barefoot again, down I step through the wet grasses to the tele-scope, the yard lit by a full moon except for the spruces like shadows, and bubbles of light acres off, houses cozy and safe. Dew sparkles on the grass, on my feet, ocean glitters in through the spruces; the night is absurdly beautiful, but I no longer can blame Rachel for doing what I have just done. Virgo, Venus, Cassiopeia, the sky—my place of reason—is infected with women and love. I stand, it seems, in a vacuum, deep space. Finally I turn the scope on Jupiter, the male God of Gods, and sight the red blotch, the blurry storm far larger than Earth which makes its way slowly across the God's belly. The night is cold, a sharp land breeze and the spruces rustling, whispering new island gossip.

"Dad?"

"Jesus Christ!" I cry. "You scared the crap out of me."

"Sorry, Dad," my boy says, giggling, coming up out of the spruces and shadows. "Look how bright it is with the moon."

"What are you doing out here?" I ask. "It's after midnight."

"I couldn't sleep," he says. "So I came out to look at the moon in the telescope."

"Why were you down in the trees?"

"I had to make a leak."

"Take a leak," I say.

"Yeah, take a leak."

"Well, come on up. I was just looking at Jupiter, but we can watch the moon."

"Are you crying, Dad?"

"Don't mind me." He is smiling as if he has caught me doing something wrong.

"It's funny," he says. "It's you instead of me. It's always me instead of you and now it's not. It's very funny." He is giggling again.

"Look, did you see any carrying on?" I ask him.

"What happened?" he says. "Who was carrying on?"

"No one," I say. "I was a little angry at Kerri and I had to yell at her."

"What did she do?"

"She was sleeping in her underwear again."

"Yeah," he says, in a very understanding voice, "that's pretty gross."

"Come here," I laugh. We sit together in the wet grass, watching the moon and the clouds bending its light.

"Look, Dad, the moon's moving in front of those clouds."

"Can't be," I say. "Which is farther away, the moon or clouds?"

"The moon," he says.

"Well, then," I say.

"It must be a UFO," he says. "Dad! It's a UFO!"

"It's an illusion," I say. "The clouds are really moving. The moon is still. It's just the way the light is."

"I like the full moon," he says, and then, very cheerfully, "I think Mom is coming home tonight, Dad."

My boy is a heartbreaker. How selfish my silence about Rachel has been.

"Listen, we can't go saying things like that, Sport."

"No, really, Dad. She's coming home."

"She's not, Sport. And we can't expect her to come back. It's the two of us now. You know, all that stuff about two for one, one for all . . ."

"But she is coming home, Dad."

It is his way to cope, of course, aided so long by my ridiculous refusal to talk about her.

"Listen, Sport, she's not coming back. Okay?"

"Okay." For some reason he is not crying, which I take not to bode at all well. Instead he tilts his head to listen to the deep, hollow ringing of a buoy a mile or two out.

"Dad," he finally says, "don't you want her to come home?"

"Okay," I say, feeling my voice give, "I do want her back. You don't know how much I want her back. Well, of course, you do. Don't you?"

"Yes," his voice wobbles.

"I know you do," I say.

"Well," he says, "isn't it at least possible? It's possible, isn't it, Dad? Anything's possible."

Those words of hers. I want to tell him that the two of us have to be more honest. Let's be honest, I want to say to him, the man who stole her has a lover's eyes, kind and gentle.

"It's something we both want," I say to my boy. We watch the moon again, moving, as it does seem, in front of the clouds. Then, finally, at the risk of losing her voice for good, of silencing her words in him forever, "We both want her to come back so much," I say, "which is why we can't go thinking it's just going to happen. Wanting it doesn't make it possible. That's not how the world works, Sport."

"So if we want it to be possible for Mom to come back, she won't?"

"Yes, well, no, but . . ."

"Come on, Dad, why won't you say it's at least possible?"

In his state and mine, I can tell we will have to leave more hits of reality for another night.

"Okay," I say, finally. "I suppose it's possible."

The sky, those trails of smoky light. I will be damned how much the moon looks like it is moving in front of those clouds.

"Come on, Dad," my boy says, now contented, "let's go in."

He tugs at my hand, and we start up the hill to our dark house, our moonlit shadows far more graceful than our tentative steps. Up the path worn into the wind-blown grass, through the wreckage of lawn chairs resting on their arms, around a patch of

Kerri's fresh cigarette butts and up onto the creaking porch. In we go, a moonlit corridor to the swaying banister, up the steps, and it all might be bearable, my boy leading me this way through the rest of it.

My boy, though, has been leading me into a false calm, into the dark hallway upstairs and a broken grasp, he to his room, me to mine. The house swallows the patter of his feet.

Alone I trek to my bedroom, back through the empty wing of the house. It is all must and night in this house. The hallways smell like the inside of attic trunks and obsolete memories. The rugs are damp, unraveling orientals. The flooring is cedar with a cavernous echo and gaps for drafts between the boards, and there always is a three-degree tilt into ocean air, into the oppressive smell of rotting shell-life and seaweed when the waves are in doldrums . . .

But it appears our house also has the stuff of great legend.

Wood sprites dance in the bedroom closets. Morpheus and Hymen swing on the drapes. Through windows propped open, the music of the spheres sails in off the night. Specters. UFOs. Pegasus mid-descent. It seems any myth you can imagine might overwhelm these old walls at any moment or charge the air in any room.

Rachel is asleep in our bed.

Holding Pattern
at D.C. National

Now it was night. It was nights before Walton got caught, finally arrested, nights before he finally let our neighborhood fall to relief and old routine. We were waiting up here on our hill for warm Jincy, Walton's lover, though Jacks and I didn't mention her, didn't even know we were waiting for her. Jacks and I had sat silent with Walton while the neighborhood brick shadows stretched down below us, turned to lamplit broken glass, took the chill off the bottles in our hands. Jincy. That afternoon, she had cut the kid loose, dropped him without a whisper, and now it was night, distant smoke in our throats, on our skin, only smells. Jacks and I had a straight view to those slow-motion pieces of light on the horizon, other people flying places, planes so slow they should have dropped. We were only waiting, watching, next to Walton the poet, wanting Jincy as much as he did in that damp night air, not knowing our own wants.

Walton's face held enough cityglow and neon from Roo's Liquor sign to show his big eyes near glassy watching nothing or everything, maybe watching the planelights even then. We couldn't see National for the distant skyline, the pitch Navy Yards silhouette, Fort McNair, then Bolling Base, but Jacks and I knew the Airport from the white lights crawling in and out. This hill we sat on was our hill, built off fallen stone and charred dust you still taste from a blazed-out slumrent, off jagged blocks of concrete and plasterboard and empty 40 bottles, and wreckage long covered over now by city smog and dirt, and brown, dead grass. The grass cover almost took out the fire smell, forgot the wreckage underneath, made it feel like we sat on a true piece of mountain. Jacks and I were always waiting up here for something we couldn't explain. In the breezes, in an hour, somebody might say her name.

This Jincy was white, see, and from outside these blocks, and somehow Walton had spun the right words for her for some time. Couple of months at least the two of them were walking around. I'm white and she's the whitest white I've seen, the inside of sunlight. Walton's a brown. Jacks is pitch, watched him get blacker with his years. Not that this is a matter as much here. This might be a last place in the city where poor is the first color. Jincy wasn't poor, she was so white.

It was getting loud down in the neighborhood with new night noise, car motors, shouts, door slam echoes. It was too cool for November, but Jacks and I weren't cold yet—the drinks. Jacks the talent lit a cigarette with a swig of St. Ide's under his tongue. He sat in night shadow, bull's chest, bolt-upright back mostly lost in the dark.

"Where do these people go?" Jacks said. More flyers crept off the orange haze into deep night.

"Anywhere," I said. "Buffalo."

Walton wouldn't make a noise. After awhile we couldn't help but imagine hearing him breathe and sweat and shiver, and we did wonder, finally—wondered still without admitting wanting her—what a new dead heart used to feel like when we were just nineteen. Once before, couple of years before, Walton had tried to kill himself when he was cut loose. He took a shoplifted bic, disposable mind you, and bungled the job. Snapped the handle, cut his arm with the jagged plastic and barely broke skin. His poetry had failed him that time, too. Those lines he wove to get this Latina off the Heights into bed with him—he must've started believing his own rhyme. Wide-eyed, hard-shouldered thinker, always under love, believing his own poetry. Magicians believing in magic ought to know better.

Jacks and I were caught up in the cityline, though, the only civilized view in the neighborhood, trying not to let the boy's dead heart crowd out a few moments of contentment with the drinks and the view. Though Jacks and I knew better about this view. From here you could see the White House if you stood. We sat. Jacks always called it other people's view, those monuments and lit memorials and dark museums, those red rooftop lights to guide in the planes, hell even the planes themselves, too. Jacks always said it was other people's so we'd drop our cold empties and head to the street for refills, or just to find home.

But this night with Walton was early still. Air traffic was heavy, we wanted to watch. We drank our false heat, with those slow horizon lights without sounds, and everything became quieter than it could be. For a moment, a whole minute, longer, we kept the quiet going. Jincy might come back. There was balance in the possibility of it, with those sharp white lights hanging mid-air out there, though Jacks and I knew better than to be caring any-more about it. A deep black cloud ceiling started rolling in. The first short night breezes came up off the rooftops raising goose-bumps we didn't feel from inside.

"She stole my windows," Walton finally said, and those quiet pearl lights that had swallowed us up spit us back out.

"What the hell you talking about, boy?" Jacks said.

"Jincy. She stole my windows."

"Jesus, boy, you always got to speak in code?"

Sitting between them I didn't want to be in the middle of this fight that was going to be about talking above your neighborhood. Jacks thought Walton's poetics was just a way of the boy trying to be more than he was, of denying he was three-quarters black and dirt broke and no better than the rest of us. Headlights coming, Roo's sign blinking split the damp shadows up the side of the hill, changed nothing up top or in the view. I knew Walton never was going to be more than neighborhood, but I didn't want him to give up his words either.

"You lose your windows," Walton said, "then you can understand."

"What the hell, boy, you think I can't get a damn metaphor or whatever? Give it up a little bit." Jacks spoke each stale word on the verge of cough. "Give your head a little peace."

My grip went tight on the bottle, almost hot in my hand with unswallowed sips. This must've been my anger I was afraid, this grip, though I couldn't tell which one of them I was angry at, couldn't find a place to sit down my bottle. But Syl showed, I was grateful. She shouted up from the street at us, broke the feeling. "James Jackson, that you?" Syl shouted.

"Yeah," Jacks yelled down to her, "come up here, Syl."

"Beirut, you there, too?"

She should've noticed me first, because Jacks was almost invisible at night, but from the street the city lights must've shown on him more than me. People always notice him first when the two of us are together, even, for no reason, in hot daylight.

"Yeah," I shouted down to Syl, "I'm here." She had her hands on her hips, wearing her "Nubian Princess" shirt you could see even from up top the hill. Something silver in her ear held storelight from inside Roo's. "Come up, Syl," I said. "Yeah, come up."

While Jacks and I watched her climbing up, hands and feet like cats', Walton must've crawled away. Once Syl was up and sitting next to Jacks, I remember worrying about Walton for a moment at first, but there was something different about this time with him. He had some little fight in him, this time, with his standing up a little to Jacks, instead of just quit in him like the other times he was a brokenheart. I let go of him. Jacks and Syl and I drank together on the wet grass, just the three of us, and took in those lights up off the skyline that seemed to defy gravity more and more. The lights seemed slower and slower, impossibly slow to keep afloat. They seemed even to stop sometimes, matted on space.

Soon Syl started treating Jacks and me like celebrities, calling us her men and squeezing Jacks's arm. Jacks knew Syl since she was twelve, hanging on laundry line like circus wire three flights over street. That was before I was dropped here, though not much before. Jacks and I weren't dealing but we weren't on our way out either. But we were good enough for Syl that night. Maybe she liked us because Jacks and I had the reputation for coming up here every night and she thought we were heavy thinkers. Syl was an easy mark for Walton with the romance she sees into people whether it's really there or not. Walton could sleep with her anytime he wanted. Maybe he already did. I was glad he slipped away because I could tell the way Syl was squeezing Jacks's arm and fingering his neck that Jacks was feeling young a little, enough to let the drinks do the rest of his feeling for him. Syl with her cajoling was relaxing him, easing those trenches in his face even though there wasn't enough light to see all his shadows loosen, see all his calm. We both felt calm with temporary Syl there. We let her occupy us, with Walton and that restlessness well gone.

"I'm shaving my head," Syl said. Her curls were cropped tight already, but she had good curves to pull it off. When Roo's sign blinked up, you could see her nipples pushing cold hard against her shirt.

"A Nubian Princess's got to do what she's got to do," Jacks said. Jacks was married once, but somebody left somebody and the story changed according to whether Jacks was on a drunk.

"She has to," Syl said.

"Beirut, we're on cash?" Jacks said to me.

"No," I said, "all we got's in these bottles."

So we saved our sips, talking for long stretches in between, listening to Syl tell about walking the Heights all drunk or knitting her Kente cap or trying to get on with Cleaning at one of the Smithsonians. She pointed at one of the long black shapes on the cityline, said that was the museum where her Aunt worked who might be able to get her an application. Her gesture was our only reminder for awhile that the rest of the city was out there. She talked about Billy's cats, creaks in her floors, smell of her mother's hot bread, even about a younger Jimmy Jackson always pleading with her to let him catch her from the clothesline. Backfires and short horn bursts echoed up from the alley-wide streets. The 295 traffic sent rumbles up to us, cracks like lightning, people driving over road joints. For awhile there was screaming like singing coming off a fire escape we could only see in shadow a block away. The neighborhood was speaking up as Syl spoke her stories. We even listened to the breezes snaking through the long grasses on top of our hill, whistling through our empties. We even heard the bell clanging on Roo's Liquor door, everybody going in to get recharged. And all this, for awhile, lured us in like massage. With just the three of us on this hill, for awhile, the neighborhood background was strangely musical and peaceful and good, even the distant screaming seemed like opera song, the best buzz and peace we had in a long time. When the singing down a block stopped, there wasn't a larger question anywhere.

Then without a warning Walton came out of the shadows, making us feel like we'd been avoiding something. Syl noticed him first. "Walton," she said, her voice singing up her excitement at seeing him, "what're you doing up here?" Walton sat next to me, opposite end as Syl, crossed his hard arms. Syl didn't leave Jacks's big arm, but she loosened her grip.

"I was up before, left for awhile," Walton said, keeping his eyes out on the night.

"Where you been?" I asked him. Jacks was wondering, too, but wouldn't ask.

"Writing," Walton said in whisper.

"To Jincy?" I said, too quickly, without thought, without knowing I'd be wondering so quickly.

"The white one?" Syl said, more kindly than she could've.

"To everybody," Walton said.

Jacks lit another cigarette, struck the match so hard it seemed the flame came from his finger tips. "Give it up, boy," Jacks said. "Whoever 'everybody' is, they won't be listening to you."

Everything peaceful left in a hurry. Jacks and Syl and I looked at our empties in hand like they might refill themselves at least by a swallow, give us a break from the silence Walton hung around our heads. The three of us started getting the cold shivers. I tried to break the quiet, tried to get Walton involved in our old conversations. "Walton's got an in, too," I said. "You know, Walton, Syl's got this aunt at Smithsonian. Is it that one, Syl?" I said, pointing to the distant black rectangle I thought she spotted out to us before.

"Yeah," Syl was helping me, "Air and Space."

"And Walton," I said, "Walton has a cousin Derrick— Derron?— who's in Baggage at National."

"Really?" Syl said. "Walton, how's your cousin get that job?"

"That's a job," Jacks said. "Baggage at National. Walton, you in with Derron?"

But Walton wasn't answering, just staring at the white points of light stuck mid-sky, the red rooftop lights showing people where they left, and the billboards way out by 295 with their backs to us. That screaming down a block on the fire escape started up again, this time louder, a woman's yells and cut more desperate, but her old iron stairwell was mostly in shadow from up where we were. Some storelight off the alley that held the escape blinked red on the old grit bricks, lit the escape a little, nothing more than black shade moving its arms and yelling, like she was yelling up to us. The yelling started echoing and bouncing, like it came from deep out of the sewers, through the manhole covers, off the rooftops, instead of from some person, still like it was meant for us. Jacks's new cigarette smoke stuck in our lungs. We didn't move. When you move, to help, the yelling disappears, always, by the time you're there, out of breath and fear. We only were a little grateful for some neighborhood misery to distract us from our own damp quiet.

"That's some dream," Walton said, dropping in cold with his words. Might've been he meant the sky sights were a dream. I hoped through that shrill screaming down a block that's how Syl and Jacks would take it. That screaming. I knew, though, Walton meant to put it on Syl for making cleaning third shift at a Smithsonian some big new prospect.

"Think baggage, boy," Jacks said, reading Walton all the way.

Down that alley a block off, somebody shined a flashlight on the screams, lit a woman. She went still. She was a black girl by herself wearing not a stitch, stuck on the escape two stories up facing us without a ladder to the street. She must've got high and had a window latch catch behind her after she climbed out. She tried to cover her chest up with her arms, cross her legs, turn away from her spotlight. Then she quit, stood there, hands at her sides, waiting.

"I'm cold," Syl said. She was never wearing enough either. The temperature was dropping faster than it should with that roof of clouds rolled in over the glow. The drinks were wearing off, it could frost.

The fire escape girl leaned on an iron rail, exposed and naked, thin, given up on hiding anything, still waiting for what was next. "I'm really cold," Syl said. With the clouds in, the sky was holding more orange citylight. Syl nuzzled herself into Jacks some more. It was hard to tell how old the black girl on the fire escape was from up on the hill—sixteen, seventeen. She stood motionless, propped on that black rail, a frozen statue, from up here. We couldn't help her staring past the flashlight, trying to see who lit her up bare.

She wasn't real.

Somebody cut their flashlight and the naked black girl was gone. We braced a little for the screaming to start up again.

"Ready, Jacks?" I said.

The screaming didn't begin back. Jacks looked straight ahead. Syl had her head down, moved a finger around the wet lip of her empty.

"Jacks, ready?" I said. I turned to Walton to tell him we would head, but in the soft orange light he was smiling, only catching the cold light off the city unless a flash from Roo's sign. I wondered what gave him any right to be so smug, like he was putting it on all of us for being mere average sprawlers. Somewhere else I would've had more the right than him but I didn't act it. I threw my empty over my shoulder. The bottle clinked, wouldn't break on something behind us. I saw only what Jacks saw in Walton, then, this smug pretender sitting himself over us. I hated him like Jacks did.

"Let's go, Jacks," I said.

"Something's wrong," Jacks said without turning to me. I thought he meant with the naked girl at first, meant that some neighbor didn't have a favor in mind for her, but she was already just deep purple afterimage.

Then I realized that Jacks and Walton both knew something, that whatever Jacks was talking about was the same thing that Walton was smiling at. Walton wasn't being all smug with his smile. He and Jacks were into something I didn't know.

"What?" I said. "Syl, you—?"

"Beirut, hush it up," Jacks said.

So we sat there and everything went quiet, no rooftop breezes even, city sounds still, as if they were silent just for Jacks.

"Something's wrong out there," Jacks said again.

"I see it," Walton said.

"Somebody give me a goddamned clue, please," I said.

"Beirut," Jacks said, "how many lights we count at most ever?"

Then I saw what they saw. One night two years before, it was high clear out and Jacks and I counted forty-one planelights coming and going from National, hanging on the view above skyline. Usually we saw eighteen or twenty planes at one time on regular nights, six, seven, less in fog. But this night, for a cold clouded night with the cityglow as strong as it gets, there were too many lights. "What?" I said. "How many are out? Forty-five? Fifty?"

"I got fifty-six," Jacks said. He'd been counting through the screaming.

Walton had, too. "I got sixty-two," he said, gesturing off right toward Bethesda and Wheaton, "counting these off pattern up North." Looking up North he had the back of his head to us, but

I knew he was still smiling. I started counting pieces of light as fast as I could.

"There's six more must be sitting out past Alexandria," Jacks said, checking South.

"What's going on?" Syl said like she'd been drifted off.

"It's the planes, Syl," Jacks said.

"What?"

"There's too many."

"Too many for what?"

"For National," Jacks said. "Planes coming in but none putting down."

"Seventy-one!" I said. "Christ, I got seventy-one."

"Seventy-four," Walton said. He had turned behind us to look out East, which never had a view but black sprawl haze, but tonight had nine more shimmers hanging mid-air. "Eighty-three," Walton said. "That's eighty-three."

"Sky's filling up," Jacks said. "Everybody's knocking, but nobody's answering the door."

"Why aren't they landing them?" Syl asked.

"It's holding patterns," I said.

"Something's wrong," Jacks said, "at National."

We watched the sky start to fill up with landing lights that wouldn't be used to land, with new stars inching into view, crowding out the sky, picking up patterns in layers over the city, and way out into the sprawl, hanging just under the high roof of clouds and as low as a few hundred feet above ground, every height in between. Some of them circled slowly at heights low enough it seemed to graze the Monument, seemed ready to land on the Mall, clip the flags off the Hill. The first engine roars, still distant and too high, began to pull us in. There were silent patterns we couldn't see, too, in the icy cloudbank and above, stretching up as far as we could imagine, everybody waiting for National to say okay, come on in.

"Let's go," Jacks said.

"What do you mean 'let's go'?" Syl said. "It's beautiful."

"Other people's view," Jacks said. "Let's go."

"It's our view," Syl said, "and it's beautiful."

"Aesthetics," Walton said, trying to be beyond us, "balanced aesthetics."

"Fools, two of you are fools," Jacks said. "Beirut, you listen to this?" Jacks was tensing me up, but he and Walton couldn't both be in the know and be dead opposites.

"What happened at National?" said Syl. "How's a view like this come up?"

"Who gives a damn?" Jacks said. "You're all three suckers. Who gives one damn?" He struck a new match to ridicule us.

But I still wanted to know. Despite all the nights Jacks talked about recognizing the skyline for other people's view, I still wanted to know what was on at National this night. The patterns for these planes were clogging up everything now, lights like pinpricks stuck on distant black, closer crisscross routes, even some visible landing gear down overhead and behind us. Some plane routes, those closest, lowest planes that expanded their patterns to over our hill and behind, were so low and close now we were starting to understand the speed in them for once, to feel the violence in the noise of their engines. Now we could understand the sheer force in the planes, how they flew so easily, and I wanted to know why everything was different tonight.

"I'm with Syl," I said. "What the hell is on at National, I want to know, and what the hell's so wrong in wondering?"

Jacks drew hard on his new cigarette, wouldn't even acknowledge us with disgust.

"Brother Jackson here won't let you think it's your city, too," Walton said, "like you got some stake in it, is what it comes back to. Right, Brother Jackson?"

"No shit, boy," Jacks said, "only without the sarcasm. You think you got stake in this town?"

"I know what's on at National," Walton said.

Jacks wouldn't bite. Syl and I were dying to ask if Walton knew what he was talking about, but Syl—Jacks scared her off any more questions. I didn't say a thing either. It was frost cold and I was hating Jacks too hard, hating him for being right, deep down I knew he was right.

"Bomb scares," Walton whispered.

"What?" Jacks said.

"National has some bomb scares over it," Walton said. Another smile broke out, lit up his eyes.

"Walton," I said, "could be anything, could be—"

"It's bomb scares," said Walton.

"How is it bomb scares?" Syl said.

"O.K.," Jacks said, "yeah, how is it bomb scares?"

A low flyer shook us for a second, the lowest plane yet, pulled rumbles behind it away off the rooftops toward National.

"Poetry in motion," Walton said. Then he laughed.

Then it all made sense.

Walton, brokenheart loverboy from the bottom of the hill, had sent one last poem to dear whiter than white Jincy, and with a few phone calls shook the stars clean out of the sky for her.

"Too many to count," Jacks whispered, his face like he was eyeing the lights out of focus, letting in the dream, "too many now."

Another low flyer scared us off our thoughts. The roars faded, boomed against each other down in the streets. Other planes flew closer. Syl shivered. The city was fireworks with the glimmers.

"That's one lucky white girl," Syl said.

"It's to everyone," Walton said. "Not just Jincy."

I sat next to plenty of thugs, dealers, users, knock-and-enter types in that neighborhood, but I was never having trouble swallowing like I was there next to Walton. He was nothing more than common crime with this stunt, except he was everything more, too, poet pretender, street poor black, governor of the town at the same time.

"Too many lights," Jacks said again, still a little lost from us, like the planes were flying around inside his head.

"How do you like it, Brother Jackson?" Walton said. "How do you like my poem?"

The air was frozen sharp. We were bracing for another plane to shake the neighborhood. Jimmy Jackson's brow doubled creases with the prospect of Walton being the true author of it all.

"You run out of paper?" Jacks said.

"You like it?" Walton said again.

Jacks tossed away his last butt still a little lit. "Yeah," he said, starting up a deep grin, "I do like it. I like it much better, now that I know who it's by."

Then, around the four of us, our hill started filling up.

Hard engine rushes carrying through alleys, landing lights dissolving street shadows, these planes shaking sky just above drew people out of Roo's and broken window panes. Somebody said National was on tv with its bomb scares. Everybody wanted to come up to see it, see the glitter pasted around the sky, feel the hill shift under engine shock. Everybody wanted to see what happened when the rest of the world had to just stop and wait, fly in circles, pray for some ground. Everybody wanted to see who did it, see how it is that one of us could have this kind of effect on scenery. Eventually the planes even stirred the old hard use out of their cracks, still holding their empty broken car antennae pipes like Teddy Bears.

We all sat on the hillside, a few dozen at first, then soon a hundred or two, taking turns congratulating Walton with back slaps and jibes and murmuring at moving sky, and Jacks laughing all the time his old thick smoker's laughs. We knew the poem for Jincy wasn't just from Walton. He meant to show her from the rest of us, too, all of us there on our hill. We didn't know quite what to do with that kind of knowledge. Later, not that night, later we'd be a little scared we ought to do something with it.

All of a sudden somebody said Roo's Liquor lights were out, and they were, which meant Roo was closed already, at nine-thirty, that even Roo was watching the stark lights crisscross near collide somewhere on the crowded hill with us. "You got some audience, Walton," Syl said to him softly. Even Roo was out here in the cold now, watching the new pinpricks blink into view, and none of these new flashes in the full sky could land. We all went quiet. Some new peace was coating us.

Then this came, at once, immediate, without warning.

Heavy helicopter roars, pounding down on the grasses, hard winds from the copter blades blowing away sound. The machine hovered for a moment, put us under the spotlight, exposed us all. Wind burnt our skin, sent the cold through bone. Syl, Jacks, me, Walton, all the rest of us on our hill, we squinted away the light, covered ourselves hoping for God, then lowered our arms, stared into the hot light. My hands were sharp white, so were everyone's. Then, just as fast, the spotlight rose and the helicopter was gone, ripping up sky behind it. Walton laughed. It started to snow. The snow wet our faces and hands, got in our eyes, we were looking up, still seeing rings from the helicopter light. We'd re-routed half the air traffic on the east coast and now it was snowing.

Jimmy Jackson stood up, alone, unnatural, the bull up on his
hind legs, stood for the first time in forever, like that night had
been forever, his bones cracking together. He pulled Syl up, too,
stretched his arms out after she was up. Only his stretching pulled
this old piece of memory from a buzz or a night on the way to
one, some moments and a lost view of Jimmy stretching that I
once saw. I remembered first walking the alley, looking up, seeing
a black girl sitting in shadow on her fire escape. She had her dress
on then, silent, nothing to think of. She smoked some joint,
watched over the rooftops in the direction of our hill. I smelled
her joint down in the street. The buildings split, I glanced up a
block. There was Jimmy Jackson, standing, stretching then too,
arms out, waving, reaching for air, making shadowy snow angels
in Roo's empty liquor lights and empty black air. Red neon
blinked out, and Jimmy Jackson was gone, then back, then gone,
black snow angel, top heavy for a moment, then nothing, just
black, only Roo's Liquor lights giving him shape. I didn't look
back to the black girl, went to drink away what I saw, lost Jimmy
in the buildings as I scuffed.

She might've seen him for a moment—just a flicker, just a
ghost, his own angel.

It was grey snowing now on our hill. Jimmy Jackson stood
still with Roo's neon out, stood against orange city sky, dark solid
as a monument. Syl swayed, Jimmy steadied her. It was quiet. Walton's poem was clearing itself up. Last shimmers roamed into
black, disappeared. I was dead cold. I thought about them finding
me the next day under a warm coat of white snow. I stared up
into the flakes swirling grey, lost all point of ground, forgot where
I was.

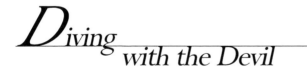

Diving with the Devil

one. *sleep*

It was early that summer and we stayed with the tourists at the resort off the beach down where the dark, lithe fishers returned each day with their lives. From the resort I often watched the sands at night blow to ashes under the moon, and the tide, deep and tossing, swallowed the stars. These nights I walked the sharp slate path cut through the obsidian. The beach opened up into fallen palms rotting in the bleached sand and the smells off the water, bloated porpoise or whale. I walked barefooted in a set of old footprints and onto the wet trunks of the fallen palms, waiting for the late westerlies to shake the casuarinas and for the tide to come in with its hushing. The near waves collapsed in slow avalanches of foam and chewed away gently at the shoreline. The crabs went dizzy in the sand. The dock swelled with the breakers off shore and thrashed like a tail, flipping severed cords and old moorings to absent skiffs, and rolling the baskets left by the men who were never guests of the smart cottages where we stayed. I was waiting for the waking dreams and the nightmares, and the nightmares that started as dreams, and it was almost like sleep. But of course, up at that time of night, amidst the prehistory and the foolish repetition of waves, I was far from sleep.

two. *the skipjack*

After hours of turning stars, the sunrise finally lit a violet wash. The first rays knifed the wavetops, and only then had the last day fallen, forgiven. I watched one of the fishermen rowing out of the horizon, ripping his oars through shadow-green sea, pulling with him that first light of day. The fisherman landed his weather-beaten boat at the dock and tied off his aft lines. His shock of hair was starkly white against the water and gloom.

This fisherman's harpoon was bent above the hooks. It was six-thirty and hot already. Already there had been a struggle at sea.

I walked out to where he had landed his boat, and the dock rose and fell under my feet with the waves. The fisherman was working a knot with his steel knife. The length of the frayed sisal rope lay at my foot by a rusted anchor. His dark hands were torn leather, and lace sheathing stitches wrapped his palms, his wrists, his black forearms. His chest and stomach drew taut as he worked.

"English?" I asked.

"A little," said the fisherman, "not too good. Español?"

"One summer a long time ago on the Guadalquivir," I said in the Spanish.

"Is not too good," said the fisherman. He had a broken tooth and a wide smile anyway.

"You're not Bahaman then?"

"No," said the fisherman.

"What are you?"

"I am not anything," the fisherman said.

"Are you Cuban?"

"San Cristòbal," he said. He dropped his knife; the old rope slid free of a tangle. "I started missing the communions there. I did not deserve them."

"Why did you leave Cuba?"

"The political," said the fisherman. "The political was very bad." He turned in his boat to collect the squirming nets. The old boat was too long for the fisherman now. The planks creaked merrily as he stepped.

"You are English?" asked the fisherman.

"American," I said.

"And the political in America is very bad?"

"Bad enough," I said.

He began to unwind a net of hot white fish. The fish were alive and drying quickly, pink mouths snapping at air. The fisherman dropped the fish into long basins full of water from which they did not try to leap.

"Would you like a cigarette?" I asked him.

"Do you have the virus?"

"No," I said. "What virus?"

"I will take nothing from a man with the virus," said the fisherman.

"I have no virus," I said. "The cigarette?"

"Sí," said the fisherman.

"What are you called?"

"Eduardo." His eyes held the ocean, changing brightly in the waves. "This is too good for American."

"It's English," I said.

"Thank you for the English cigarette. And what do they call you?"

"Peter Cole."

"I am grateful to meet you, Peter Cole. I rarely am able to meet Americans. The rest of them seem to outsleep you."

A morning fog began to rise, burning off the sea. The air was still, salt- and blood-smelling. The fisherman's harpoon hooks were encrusted deep black.

"Eduardo," I said, "tell me about the big one that got away."

"What do you say?"

"By the state of your harpoon and the tangled lines—the big one that got away. Like the famous tale in the book."

"Is a very old story, the one that got away," said the fisherman. "I rather speak of the one that did not get away. Is a very old story, too, but I like to tell it much better."

"Tell it?" I asked.

"Not today." The fisherman smoked quickly and ignored cancer and effect, staring past the morning horizon while his hands worked the netting.

"How long have you been here, Eduardo?"

"Three years," said the fisherman.

"By boat?"

"By this boat," said the fisherman. The mast was naked and splintered.

"You rowed from San Cristòbal in this boat?"

"I had a sail then."

The breeze had died. The sun was full, resting above the water. The sky turned high blue and the early day began to hold the smell of the live fish.

"Would you like another cigarette?" I asked.

"The virus will kill you," said the fisherman.

"Is it fever? I have no virus."

"Worse than fever. I saw it rot slowly a man's soul from the inside once."

"I do not have a fever."

"Yes, I would like another English cigarette."

When the basins were full and the nets empty, the waves finally calmed to steel blue. I stepped onto the boat with him and together we rolled the heavy netting and beat the harpoon with an old blacksmith's iron and made it true again. The netting was woven mesh and steel leader and in the sweat fiercely cut my fingers at the joints. The bow planks held the fish oils and stench of yesterday's kill. The old boat's flayed paint swirled white in the oils. The fisherman's dark skin kept dry while we worked.

"Eduardo," I said, "you left Cuba very late."

"I left San Cristòbal a young man, but not for here," he said. "I told you. The political was very bad."

"The Communism."

"We should have been so lucky to have the Communism. I am afraid the Communism is just a rumor."

"I'm afraid it is more than a rumor."

He shook his head. "They speak as if there will be revolution, but I do not foresee it. Who will stand against Fulgencio?"

He sat astride the center plank and held the oar handles in his lap and smoked. He was quite satisfied his catch was safe for this time in the basins. He had been missing in time and thought Fulgencio Batista still held dictatorship over his homeland.

"No," he said, "who will stand against Fulgencio?"

"Where have you been these last forty years, Eduardo?"

He let the oars settle into the water. He stood and flicked a wrist at the white horizon. "Nowhere," he said. "Fighting the conspiracy of the tides."

It was seven-thirty now, and my divemates soon would be up looking for me for breakfast. The fisherman settled again, still smoking against his mast.

"Y tú," he said. "What of you, Peter Cole?"

"What of me?"

"Why are you to south of Exuma Cays?"

"For the dives," I said.

"The dives."

"You disapprove."

"Sì, muy."

He rose and climbed on dock to the basins. "You will carry these with me up to Advena Maris?"

"They buy them?"

"Some."

"What of the rest?"

"I ride them to the Clarence Town with the waiter always deep into hangover. Today the mail boat comes in and I sell the fish when he goes to pick up the mail."

We began to walk a basin up the shore and sand. The sand gave way under foot and the battle was against our weights and the weight of the basin until the gravel road.

"The fish are more tired than we are," said the fisherman.

"Especially the marlin," I said.

"Yes," he said, laughing through a cough. "The bluefin have quit."

"Tell me. Why are you against diving, Eduardo?"

"I am not anything. Why does it matter?"

"It does," I said.

"I would like another cigarette."

"I would like to set this basin down."

We rested the basin on the gravel. The fisherman took a light and drew. "You eat fish?" he asked me.

"Of course."

"I am not the hypocrite. Pick up the basin."

We struggled slowly again toward the Advena Maris, the whitewashed walls and sharp greys, the sharp stone paths.

"I am not a hypocrite," I said.

"I eat fish, too," the fisherman said, "pero I do not get in the water and play with them."

"We do not play."

"You must have some peace below with the blue swirling above you and the sea life putting on their show for you."

"It's a partnership," I said.

The fisherman spat around his cigarette. "Oh, partnership. A sea turtle once took a bite of my rudder. You can not see a good fight when you see one."

My shoulders drawn taut, arms knotted, the basin's weight and the measured steps opened the cuts in my fingers from the nets again.

"In these basins is the first fight of the day. Not the first. The first was a great one and got away. The oldest story and such. But the second and third and the rest we carry. I know a good fight."

"It was a very heavy fight," I said.

We finally set the basin down by the jeep. The fisherman sank his brown thick hands into the water and handed me a foot of skipjack.

"Squeeze it tightly," he said. "These tuna are personal when they are caught."

I held it around the gills and the hard pounding heart. The oils began to seep into the cuts in my hands.

"Thank you for the English cigarettes," the fisherman said.

"Thank you for the skipjack."

"I crossed the Tropics of Cancer this morning for him. It was too calm."

"He will not trouble you any more," I said.

"He will trouble you."

"I will have him to breakfast."

"Eat him instead."

I went around the kitchen by the gardens and found the hung-over waiter. I gently asked him to prepare the tuna for a breakfast. When I crossed around to the dining room, the fisherman waved and grinned. "Do not have the virus," he called.

"I don't," I said and returned his wave. "So long, Eduardo." I was calling too loudly for the hour.

"Peter Cole," he called.

My hands smelled unpleasantly. Inside the early risers ate quietly.

"Peter Cole."

"Yes?"

"Do not think I do not know of Fidel Castro very well," said the fisherman.

I went to wash my hands.

Inside the breakfast room the hung-over waiter startled me from concentrating on a two-week-old *Times*. The room smelled like cinnamon and smoke. The *Times* had been opened, which meant that already my divemates were around looking for me. The waiter was a Bahaman who didn't braid, or wash the sunlight out of his eyes. He was always squinting. He asked if I wanted frittered conch with my breakfast and I told him that I had been there two weeks and had eaten conch everything twice already. Would I like to try an egg? No, I was fine. And today the stewed tomatoes were a treat? I was fine. He brought me some toast that I didn't eat and we agreed without speaking of it to a truce. Then he brought me the skipjack and I ate it quickly.

three. *old kiss*

Jen, Matt, Lawrence, and I had gone to the secluded Newton's Cay to spend another day waiting out the first dive of the season. The divemaster hadn't yet flown onto the Island, and there was no telling how long the wait would last. Jen and I swam and snorkeled warm shallows over the red coral so close to shore. She had on her yellow suit again, and we stayed within arm's reach.

Matt was spin casting from the beach with a rod he had found in a shed at the Advena Maris. He was hoping for swordfish that were going to wander in close enough to the beach because he had heard a story once. He leaned into each cast off a split knee that had cut short a Second Division contract at Bristol Rovers the year before we met at school. When he walked he still limped. He had thick wrists, though, and cast easily for distance. Jen and I watched the sinkers splashing ahead of us in the water and the fish ignoring his line.

Lawrence poured drinks and sat in the white sand, sweating and red out of breath, fighting sand fleas and swearing. He wore white shorts and white knee socks and a bulging white shirt stuffed into his shorts. Matt had told him at breakfast that he looked about to go on safari. We had only met Lawrence a couple years before, in St. Simons. He was ten or twelve years older than us, and we overlooked many things for him.

The cuts in my hands from the fisherman's nets had dried thinly and darkened in the sun until I went in swimming. No one mentioned them until Jen did much later in the day. The water was arrhythmic, the waves breaking and swelling like skipping heartbeat over coral and shallow beach. Jen and I, floating, were only spending away the afternoon. Once we heard a purr through the water and then saw Fitch's white plane directly overhead of us, a glint in blue sky. Fitch was the only pilot on and off Fernandina, and he was supposed to be flying the divemaster in.

"Where's he going, Pete?" Lawrence asked from the beach. "I thought he was supposed to be going to Hopetown for the divemaster."

"He is," I said.

"Hopetown's north," Lawrence said, pointing west.

"Petey, what's Lawrence pointing at?" Jen whispered.

"Something around Lisbon, I think." She and I were standing together in the shallows. Her bangs left a wispy shadow on her forehead, her eyebrows, gave her cat's eyes.

"Lawrence," Matt said, "why don't you go bag us an elephant or something."

Lawrence grumbled and smacked an invisible flea on his thigh.

"Hopetown's that way," I said to Lawrence, pointing along the line of white shore.

"Well, that's still not how he's going," Lawrence said.

"It's not your fault, Lawrence," Matt said. "They keep switching it around."

"It's nice to see the plane still flies," Jen said. "I was beginning to wonder." The single-prop dropped out of sight below a row of dried palms.

"Elephants beware," Matt said. "Lawrence is on the blood spoor."

Late in the afternoon Jen and I were standing again in the clear water when we kissed once on a joke openly in front of Matt. He only laughed at us and cast again. She had offered the dare. "Now," she said, a yellow strap lazily off one shoulder, "now, with Matthew watching us." Her shoulders were glistening in the heat. She gave me a blue wink and I remembered all the reasons there might be to love her. It was a very old kiss. She took my hands in hers, turned my palms into the sunlight as if she'd tell my fortune.

"I was helping a fisherman this morning."

"Early?" she asked.

"Yes."

"Don't you ever sleep anymore?" she asked.

"An hour is all I can stand for," I said.

"Petey."

"It's okay." I told her. "The sun will dry them out again." The cuts had been fine in the saltwater but now the air was hitting them and they were shooting. Her eyes were bursting coronas, though. I was looking at her too long.

Matt hit everything too hard the rest of the day. He lost 200 yards of tackle and half his sinkers to unnamed fish, but we were all, except for Lawrence, only semi-drunk and forgiving. We were drinking our drinks for some reason out of copper cups Matt had taken from Advena Maris, which we eventually found funny and reason to pose like Norsemen. After awhile the deep blue Exuma Sound and then the outside Atlantic found us, and the waves breaking in our heads, and then a plum-red sunset. Jen and Matt went to find a place away in the sand and left me alone with Lawrence and the decaying light. Lawrence, after a day drinking in the sun and sitting in one place in the sand, was loaded.

four. *the limp and the breezes*

Lawrence did not sober up after dinner. Back in the room he lay on his bed in his dinner clothes. He had forgotten to brush away the dead palmetto bugs. He was well over his weight and couldn't catch his breath, even with the small room open to the breeze. I told him I was going out.

"Where to, Pete?"

"Anywhere," I said.

"There's only the bar," he said.

"I know."

"Bring me a tart," he giggled.

"You've been watching black and white movies again," I said. "Besides, there's not a tart on the Island, except for the one Matt's got."

"What did she mean by kissing you like that, Pete?"

"Nothing," I said. "She meant nothing."

"That's fine," he said. He closed his eyes.

"Good night, Lawrence."

"Good night, Pete."

"I'm going to leave it unlocked."

"And Pete?"

"Yes?"

"I'm too tired for a tart," he giggled again.

"No more bad movies."

I went to the bar. The bartender who understood me was off that night and a local couldn't find the good stuff. I sipped a local rum with some kind of peppery kick to it and began to wait out the night.

It had been falling dusk when Jen and Matt had left me alone with Lawrence up at the Cay. The air was turning back to the ocean then, an agreeable twilight having passed, the day turning to black and white. Jen was arching her back, loosening her top, her breasts falling bare to the sea air. She was whispering to Matt a little too loudly how wonderful he had been the night before. I used to be sure she would leave him worse off than she had me. The two of them strolled away to the cadence of his limp and the breezes. Though she wouldn't marry him, they had been together eleven years now, and evidently she was done using up men.

five. *the only pilot*

Several days passed and the dives were postponed because the divemaster didn't come in. I went down to the dusty excuse for a runway one morning before breakfast to find Fitch to ask him about it.

Fitch was a redhead from Chicago who had been the only pilot on and off Fernandina for twenty-four years. He used to scare Christ out of people doing stunts in the old single-prop on the way in. He quit the stunts after a close call he wouldn't talk about. They would have taken his license for the close call, but he had no license to begin.

"If you're here about the stunts, Mr. Cole, I don't want to talk about it."

"I'm not here about that."

He sat in the plane looking at the registry and drinking from a bottle with the label ripped off. The registry, torn into disarray, was a formality for some official from Nassau.

"I don't do them anymore," Fitch said, "those stunts. It was a hell of a thing to do anyway."

"It was," I said. "You scared the soul out of us when we came in last month."

Fitch laid the registry on the seat. "I remember," Fitch said. "Go away." The bottle was making his eyes water.

"I wanted to apologize for Lawrence," I said.

"The fat guy who tossed up the side of the plane."

"Yes."

"Don't."

"Why not?"

"Don't apologize," he said. "He's the only one of you with any sense. You ought to be pretty damned scared to fly in a rickety old single-prop, Mr. Cole. I just wish he didn't do it up the side of the plane."

"We're sorry about that."

"What is he, Scottish?"

"Canadian."

"You want to hear the story?" Fitch said.

"Okay."

"Well, I'm not telling it," Fitch said. "It's personal, having the goddamned Christ scared off you."

A wind kicked dirt up the runway. It had yet to rain for the season. "How do you get enough lift before those palms?" I asked.

"It wasn't on a take-off if that's what you're getting at, Mr. Cole."

"Into the wind?"

"Yes, you go into the wind, Mr. Cole."

"Ever have any trouble with those winds?" I asked.

"I'll be goddamned, Mr. Cole, if you get me to talk about it."

"Okay."

"You're goddamned right it's okay, Mr. Cole."

"Why—?"

"Why do I fly?" he said. "It's pretty much just a couch if I don't fly her, Mr. Cole. Now go away, please."

"Okay."

"Every tourist is coming in with some request as if I'm the key to world peace. Save us, Fitch, save us. I've got goddamned things to do."

"I understand."

"Like hop to Hopetown to get the goddamned divemaster. Plus I like to drink in peace."

"He's coming in then?"

"If he meets the damn plane this time. He left me there two hours yesterday with my pants down drinking rum. I hate waiting and I hate rum."

"What's that?"

"It's rum. You thirsty?"

"Okay."

"What do I care if the goddamned divemaster meets the plane? I get paid either way. Old Rainer's a sport." Rainer was the old Austrian with thin eyes and a wide face who ran the Advena Maris. Fitch was the only person I ever had met who liked him. "I'd be careful with that divemaster, Mr. Cole."

"We've all taken dozens of dives before," I said. "Plenty with poor divemasters."

"I'll need to get that bottle back, Mr. Cole."

"Sorry." I was out of cigarettes. The others would be looking for me soon.

"You're restless without the dives, Mr. Cole."

"I'm a little restless."

"It's why I do half the crap I do," said Fitch. He took up the rum again.

"Like fly?" I asked.

"Yeah," Fitch said. "Sure."

"I'm sorry. I shouldn't have been asking you about all that."

"It's understandable," Fitch said. "You're without the dives, Mr. Cole. I was looking to talk to someone anyway."

The palms at the end of the runway shook for a second. I turned to go. "Don't get the virus," I said.

"I wouldn't say that if I were you, Mr. Cole."

"Say what?"

"About the virus," Fitch said. "You shouldn't be talking about that."

"It's just something someone said to me," I said.

"You're just a tourist, Mr. Cole. I wouldn't go around saying anything about it."

"It's just a line," I said. "It's only something heard."

"Well, don't repeat that kind of thing, Mr. Cole. You could get into some things you don't want to."

"Like what?"

"Like quit asking," Fitch said. "I'm doing you a favor here, Mr. Cole. You're just a tourist. Don't talk about it anymore."

"I won't," I said.

"It's understandable, Mr. Cole. You're without the dives."

six. *The Bight*

It was Matt's idea to kill the day jeeping down to the Bight. After an hour on the sand and root road we had yet to reach the old Spanish church ruins. The morning glories were out, dizzy from the jostling jeep. The heat and the swirl grew familiar. We drove through the inland salt dunes where Diamond Salt stored the salt until they shipped it. The company was much farther south and the salt dunes up here were deserted and shifting under their own weight, crackling as the grains ran down the slopes. We passed chickens in yards of tall grass and shacks without windows, the screen doors hanging off their hinges or smacking closed on springs as we sped by. Then the land finally turned to deep weed and shade, and then, finally, the Spanish ruins, collapsed blackstone blocks, windblown and rounded, the roof long fallen in. The blackstone soaked away sunlight. The floor of the old church under the fallen roof never saw anything more than shadow. We walked the cobbled steps through the fallen stones silently for some time, the high black walls and thick windows of shaded arches above us, out onto the crushed grey shells and the strewn rubble. We walked out to see the jagged tide going out quickly on the Atlantic, soon again to turn back in. We were waiting for Matt to get wrecked enough to head back to the Advena Maris. He had his own bottle, quickly drinking as he always did the day before we started a season's diving. The waves, though not distant, didn't drum very noisily against the beach. Only the dead shells snapped as we stepped. Even Lawrence was silent.

We finally sat on the cold stones inside the walls on the remains of the old roof. The stone inside had piled high enough to see through the arch windows to the dark ocean and whitecaps and the clouds rolling in. We were always alone when we came here.

Lawrence asked Matt for a drink. Jen sat between Matt and me, a blanket across her lap and mine. She wore her yellow bikini and slouched.

"Is there a good divemaster, Petey?"

"I suppose," I told her, despite what Fitch had said.

"I had one in Lesser Antilles put out empty tanks for everyone," Matt said.

"We were there," Jen said. "We didn't even get into the water that day, Matthew."

"I was talking to Lawrence, wasn't I?"

"What was that?" Lawrence said.

"Nevermind," Matt said.

"There's a virus about," I said. The mood was more agreeable to distract Matt by worrying Lawrence.

"A virus?" Lawrence piped.

"I'm immune," Matt said.

"How do you know?" Lawrence asked him.

"I'm immune to everything."

"He is," Jen said. "I don't think I've ever seen you sick." He was immune to everything, except the day before the first dive.

"How do you know there's a virus, Pete?" Lawrence asked.

"A fisherman warned me of it," I said.

"The same one who cut up your hands, Petey?"

"When did you start keeping with fishermen?" Matt asked.

"We've got to find you some sleep," Jen said.

"Could this fisherman be telling you wrong?" Lawrence asked, still fixated on his fear of disease.

"I don't think so," I said. "Fitch knew of it, too."

"Then, it must be true," Lawrence said.

A breeze swept for a moment, smell of salt. We watched the clouds pass across the sun and whiten it.

"It looks like the center of a dead eye," Matt said.

"I hate this place," Jen said.

"I'm going to ask Rainer about this virus," Lawrence said.

"I wouldn't do that, Lawrence."

"Why not, Pete?"

"Because local owners are always touchy about things like that."

"I see very scabby boils in your future, Lawrence," Matt said, "and fever blisters in hard-to-reach places."

"I'm definitely going to Rainer," Lawrence said.

"You don't listen," Matt said. "Pete told you not to."

"Well, why does it have to be a big secret, Pete?"

"It's business," I said.

"Business?"

"When those cute little coastal towns in Maine don't tell about shark attacks, it's business," Matt said.

"Have they had shark attacks here, too?" Lawrence asked.

"Not since this morning," Matt said.

"Are you joking, Matt, or are you serious?"

"Take it easy, Lawrence," I said.

"Don't worry, Larry," Jen said, "it's nothing to do about it now."

"Pete, are they kidding?"

"They're kidding, Lawrence."

"Look on the sunny side," Matt said, "if a shark hits you Lawrence, you're cured of the virus."

"I'm talking to Rainer," Lawrence said.

"Lawrence, don't," I said. "We're in cozy with these people as far as the dives and the rooms."

"I don't think our room's so hot, Pete."

"Well, it is. It's a palace compared to the others, so please leave Rainer out of it."

"Don't bring up the sharks to him either," Matt laughed.

"Matthew, I know there aren't any sharks," Lawrence said.

It was not to say.

Matt was drunk enough now. Jen reached for my arm under the blanket. Matt opened a second bottle.

"There aren't any sharks?" Matt asked.

The sun had moved off us. The church smelled its age and damp. Matt had spent the day avoiding nothing and the gin making it worse, and now Lawrence was telling him there was nothing to fear. It made little difference that Matt had baited him.

"Have you ever been hit by a shark, Lawrence?"

"Look, Matt, I know that you have, and—"

"No, not me. I have only been able to see it in person."

He had quieted Lawrence for good now and was thinking about how to salvage his day, drinking the second bottle as quickly as he could. He handed the halved bottle to Jen, but he wouldn't make eye contact with her. The tide was coming in, finally. Finally we heard the surf pound and crack. Matt's eyes lit.

"I'm going for a swim," he said. "With the sharks."

"Matthew?"

"It'll be fun," he said, and bent to kiss her head. "Anybody coming? Lawrence? No? Lawrence the Great Watcher. Okay, then, meet you here in a couple of hours."

"Is this a bright idea?" I asked him.

"You must know it is, Pete." He took the bottle back from Jen. "I'll take my own companionship."

We could see the waves with the new tide more clearly now, whitecapped and tossing. The afternoon sky had turned to coal. Matt limped down to the arched door, shells crackling at his feet. I had seen him run once. It was as if the limp were a decoy and he was happy that everyone know the truth. Sometimes, the limp was like a fraternity jacket he had trouble taking off.

He peeled away his shirt and the sun caught him for a moment, a wiry frame; then the light turned grey again. He would go out a half-mile at least to make sure he was tempting the sharks fairly and then swim in with the tide.

"Be careful," Jen called.

But he was already over the banks. We weren't worried about him anyway. He could outswim most sober men drunk. One afternoon he and I swam a mile and a half off Swansea to freedive to a shallow shipwreck we had only bare boated to before. We used to be fairly easy swimmers, and with the tide having turned to come in there was little to worry about now. He seemed sometimes the only one of us with nothing really to fear.

seven. *beauty and misery*

With Matt gone for his swim, Lawrence struggled off on his own with a cigarette to think. There was nothing to do but pass the time. Jen had Gauloises and I hadn't smoked them since the Fall before in St. Simons. She laid her head against my shoulder and I kissed her on the cheek, but it was only friendly. Later the four of us would take the jeep back. Lawrence would drive the coastal road and Matt would sleep, finally, and Jen and I would warm ourselves on each other in the back. The sun would turn and bloody the beach and the water and touch off the sky. I wouldn't care that I wasn't going to sleep that night. But now there was nothing to do but pass the time.

Jen and I left the breeze for a corner down in the blackstone and a roaring shadow, surrounded by the dark sinking corners and the open roof which still shed so little light, and the time's wreckage and devastation and dirt, the misery. We sat alone, my hand between her shivering knees, her cold hands squeezing my arm under the blanket. She hated the Bight, but it was the most beautiful place I had ever seen.

eight. *eyes above night ocean*

The next morning before diving, the Advena Maris seemed full for the season. Several waitstaff and bellhops were busying themselves, readying for a big breakfast. The dining room smelled of hot bread and poached eggs and batter for waffles. It was seven-thirty, still cool in the dining room with the windows opened again to the brisk air. An elderly couple in white sat on the terrace like clouds.

Lawrence was trying to buy out from under me the house in St. Simons where Jen and Matt and I lived. "Isn't my offer adequate?" he asked.

"No," I told him.

"We both know it is, Pete."

"It's going to be very hot out on that boat, Lawrence. I wouldn't wear that jacket." By ten it would be over ninety, and it didn't bode well that his skin was the color of real butter. "If you get heatstroke, they'll cut short the dive to turn back for you."

"Everyone's tired of St. Simons anyway, Pete. Sell the house to me."

There we had the old porches and unreliable fans and afternoons of dives, as many as we could space in a week when the depths and the times permitted to avoid decompression, some of the dives very good, the evenings of the various French cigarettes brought over by an old girlfriend of Jen's, and the long walks on the beach with the troller lights fearful and floating like eyes above night ocean. We had little right to be tired of it.

"Why do you want to buy now?" I asked.

"I told you, Pete, to retire."

"At forty-six."

"Look, Pete, Matt was right."

"About what?"

"About that I'm a watcher. I watch things. I'm going to make it official is all, drop any pretext of having some type of career or ambition. And I need your house."

"Why?"

"To entertain."

"What for? Your house is a mile away from ours."

"But yours has the porches and the yards and everyone is used to dropping in there."

"What if we just promise to come by more often?"

"Look, Pete, if it'll work, it'll be at your beach house."

We couldn't find the hung-over waiter, and another Bahaman took orders. Lawrence was having only fruit to pre-empt the sea sickness he would get later anyway.

"You know I can't sell it," I told him. "It's sentimental to Jen. It's a home to her. When her father sold it to me I promised him for her I wouldn't sell it. When she was growing up in the Canal Zone and all over it was the one place they kept to vacation."

"It's a very old house, Pete, and she did leave you for Matt."

"I remember that part," I said.

"Doesn't that serve to invalidate your contract then?"

"I'm not looking to invalidate any contract," I said.

nine. *Obeah*

While Lawrence went to find Jen and Matt after breakfast, I went to the dock where I had found the fisherman called Eduardo, but nobody had seen him for several days. Then the cabana boy who was always hanging around the cabanas bringing extra towels trying to see everything and waiting for tips told me that they had seen the fisherman in Rum Cay a few days before, and that it was a wonderful catch he brought in, enough to feed Clarence Town for a week. I thanked him and he went back to throwing stones at the waves. Our diveboat was to leave from Rum Cay in an hour, but the fisherman surely would be up the coast by now with the Caribbean side winds today. The winds might get the birds out to show him where the big fish were and make an easy day of it.

I met the others at the Advena Maris garden, and yesterday had vanished from Matt. Jen was already in her green wetsuit again, dressed early to wear nothing underneath. She was quiet at his arm, her hand in the curls on his neck. Matt was clear-eyed and fearless again.

We jeeped down to Rum Cay on the only paved road on Fernandina. The heat was coming up quickly. Matt was clowning and taking the whole road, wearing his "Mad Cow look." He had driven this way the week before up at Adderly, the old slave burial grounds, and had hung us up in a ditch. Though he was trying not to show it, he was being more careful this time. The palms became sparse in the smell of seaweed and newly dead shells. The Cay was green and clear, fragile with several small boats teetering on shallow water, a sheet of green glass. On low tide the boats would rest on damp sand.

We found our gear set out on the docks and met a French couple who would dive with us. They had taken it up together only recently. The man had a hand in his hair and was as nervous as his wife who kept shifting her stance, though he was trying very hard to hide it. Jen gave them each Gauloises and the taste of home calmed them. Matt and I changed to wetsuits on the dock despite the heat, expecting to be in the water soon enough. Each of us fitted the BCDs and tried the regulators. The tanks were old but it didn't mean anything if they had been well kept. We all belted the weights except for me. Matt took two pounds and Jen took twelve. It irritated Matt that I didn't need the counterweights because he was the athletic one. The fins were brand new and we each used our own fitted masks. All in all it was pretty good gear if the tanks had kept well.

The Austrian boy who must have been Rainer's son by the same wide face and slight eyes made several trips to get the tanks on board. He was quite strong and worked barebacked. His back quivered each time he hefted a tank. The dive boat was eighteen feet, not what Lawrence had expected, though it was the largest boat in the Cay. In St. Simons they took us out on a thirty-footer and the waves were not as bad to him. He still hadn't taken off his jacket, and now the heat already had him out of breath. In the shade in the false cabin he found a seat and took out his flask.

We sat in the boat and waited for the divemaster, who was late. A good one is never late, and only the French couple and Lawrence didn't care.

"Who is this divemaster?" Matt asked Rainer's boy. The boy's irises shrank as if he were never asked questions. "Where's he from?"

"He is from Cayenne originally and now from around here," the boy said with thick Austrian stresses.

"Does he speak French?" the small Frenchwoman asked.

"Yes," said Rainer's boy. This seemed to delight her.

"Where in hell is he?" Matt asked.

"He is doing his religion this morning. He will be here in a short time. I will not rush him."

"Why can't he be rushed?" Matt asked him. "The damned dive was scheduled for ten. It's half past and there's no sign of him. He'll have us out there in the heat of the day."

"I do not rush him," the Austrian boy said.

"Why?"

"He is Obeah." The boy was tired of tourists and pleased with his answer. Jen climbed quickly out of the boat for a smoke. I followed her.

"What is Obeah?" the Frenchwoman wanted to know. Her husband was now showing the nerves much more than she and couldn't find a place to rest his elbow.

"That's just fine," Matt said, and he started to laugh. "I've always wanted to dive with the devil. The nearest I've come is diving with you, Pete."

"What is Obeah?" the Frenchwoman asked again. Her husband was speaking French to her quickly as Jen and I left. We stepped around the lizards and stood smoking on the dock in where it met shore. This was not the way to spend a summer diving.

"What do you say, Petey? Pretty good start?"

"Yes," I told her. "If he's an hour later it'll be perfect."

"And the tanks could be full of helium," she said, "if everything goes according to plan."

"And Lawrence might grab the wheel and steer her into a hidden coral on the way back," I said, "if we've got any real luck."

ten. *hypoxic incident*

When Jen and I boarded the boat again somebody had explained to the Frenchwoman about West African slavers, ritual voodoo, and vengeance as an art. She was now quite curious about the divemaster instead of afraid and felt it was now time to tell us her name was Claire. We remembered because she had told us on the dock. Her husband sat up with Lawrence chatting French or what passes for it in Canada. It was clear the Frenchman had taken up dives only for his wife. He would be the least comfortable under, and the most dangerous, and I didn't want to dive with him.

At eleven-thirty the divemaster, without a wetsuit, finally came on board. He was as dark as the deeper ocean floors and wore a black leather swim suit. His eyes were feral, only pupil and iris, with lids ready to flash hate. The long hook of an old fungal scar crossed one of his shoulders. "Go," he told Rainer's boy, and the boy jumped to his feet to take the boat out of the Cay.

I had met Obeah before and knew if you extended them consideration and courtesy they would return it, and if you didn't they would have little concern for you, and no mercy. Matt knew this as well as I, but he didn't want to spend the summer diving with only the polite version of the devil. "Where the hell you been?" he asked him, and gave a wink to the Frenchwoman, but the divemaster already had climbed to the bow to sit apart from us.

On the way out we took up depth charts with Rainer's boy and marked out our course. We were heading out into Exuma Sound westnorthwest of Cape Santa Maria to a reef forty-two feet down but that rested on a shelf that fell away three hundred. We could see a single lemon shark or two but the sharks never grouped there. Without glancing at the charts the boy kept us in a very narrow channel for several miles. The water was green, and then blue, violet, and then very clear. The breeze and mist from the boating spelled us from the heat.

We checked our gear again and decided how to pair off. Lawrence, of course, wasn't diving. The French couple wanted to dive together, as could Jen and I, and Matt then could go in with the divemaster. We decided to split it up by experience, though, since it was apparent the French couple weren't going to get much guidance from the divemaster. I would go with Claire, and Jen with the husband. This seemed something to calm him. He seemed finally to remember he was a Frenchman and introduced himself as Paul, and kissed her hand. But with Jen, really, he was like a boy with his mother. It was forty more minutes to the site. I rested in the stern with the rhythms of the pitching boat and the motor.

At the dive site we anchored in a choppy current. Lawrence was going to have a time of it. He took off his jacket and his shirt underneath was wet through. He saw his flask almost empty.

"Oh, dear," he said.

"It's probably better," I said.

"I suppose you're right, Pete."

"Just don't look at the sky or the boat floor," I told him.

"Right."

"Keep your eyes on the waves. Let your body see why it's moving this way."

"Right, Pete. That'll help."

But he would have been miserable anyway if the French-woman Claire hadn't had several drams for him. They might not work out the sea sickness, but they would let him sleep for awhile. For a Canadian who had trouble in the heat in St. Simons, he took these latitudes as personal insults. The rest of us got our gear on.

"Another bet?" Matt asked.

"Sure," I said.

"You can't beat Petey," Jen said.

"I will today," he said.

"Petey doesn't breathe."

"What do you mean he cannot breathe?" Claire asked.

"What is it, Petey, what's it called?"

"Hypoxic incident," I said.

"We all know about the famous hypoxic incident," Matt said.

"Why doesn't he breathe?" Claire said.

"You'll never beat Petey," Jen said. "He's needed less air than the rest of us since birth."

"The gauges on these tanks might not be too precise any-way," I said.

"An excuse," Matt said. "Come on, Pete. The man who uses more air pulls the anchor up by hand."

"Okay."

"That is a good bet," Rainer's boy said. It was his job ordinarily to pull up the anchor.

eleven. *narcosis*

The divemaster finally joined us at the sitting stairs to the water. "Thirty minutes," he said. He spoke with the French-dialected accent of Cayenne and without meeting eyes with anyone but Matt. "If you wish to dive at the next site this afternoon," he said, "do not follow down the shelf. The depths will be impossible to regard and unhealthy for repeating a dive later." He took his BCD and tank barebacked and went in first.

I went in next and helped Claire in with my arms at her hips. Her husband was occupied with Jen. The water was cool and clear to one-hundred, one-twenty, at least, and the reef forty below was alive already with reds and deep violet, and spots of yellow. Claire and I went under then, free from surface air, only hearing our own breathing. Her hair spread like a blond man-o-war. We began to follow the anchor line down.

At ten feet she paused again before I did to equalize and I knew she'd be safe to dive with. We watched the divemaster's dark legs, sinuous up in the surface water, and the others came in, Jen and Paul first. Paul moved very slowly in the water as if Jen had him all calmed down. From underneath we could see the boat pitching and I hoped Lawrence slept. Claire and I felt our ears clear and went down to equalize again. At twenty feet down, Matt came in and the divemaster swam to join him at the anchor line above Jen and Paul at ten. Watching them all silently going deeper I felt we would each be safe. I began to realize the bright coral below and the silver barracuda school swimming in the light like sparks.

After descending and equalizing five or six times more, Claire and I began to swim freely. With adjustments, the BCDs kept us off the coral, rising and falling slightly, slowly, only with each breath. The soft rush of bubbles with our breathing made us regard all that noise before, up and out on the surface. The teethy smirks of the barracudas didn't alarm Claire and I knew it would be easy diving with her. I let her lead slightly, staying two arms away and readily in sight with a half turn of her head. The amberjack and almaco jack, rainbow runner and yellowtail darted and were schooling and moving like fingers on the same hand. We watched a white marlin with its tailfin bitten limp along the bottom and the bottom fish motionless in sleep. The heavy water and the pressure against my chest, the new tightness of the wetsuits-there with Claire waiting out the nights alone on the dock down from Advena Maris was only distant thought.

She only froze once. A red-striped coral snake wound though a section of gold coral skeleton and she grabbed my hand. I gripped her hand back and she turned to me. I crossed my index fingers to tell her she was right to let it pass. She gave me a to-the-surface thumb. I shook my head and she was relaxed the rest of the way to the shelf.

We caught the first look off the reef down the shelf to pitch black. I was hoping for a lemon shark when Matt tapped me from behind and startled Claire. He turned up his palms to ask where the divemaster was. Matt wouldn't have left a divemate underwater and I knew the divemaster must have swum from him very suddenly. But the divemaster was nowhere in sight, which meant he already must have been far off, given the good visibility. You could tell by the look of him that he freedove and went with scuba frequently and was no one to worry for. I pointed to the water between us to tell Matt to stay but he wanted to join the others and turned. I caught his leg with my hand. He turned quickly back. I could see through his mask he was irritated, having been bothered already by the divemaster's taking off on him. I motioned to my tank. I pointed for Claire to the thin stream of bubbles coming from the center of his tank. She kept her head and I sent Matt to the top for a spare. I checked my watch. We were twenty minutes in. Claire and I checked each other's gauges and tanks while Matt swam off. We were only slightly down the shelf, say sixty feet, but if you run dry without knowing it's coming it's plenty of ocean to float through.

Claire and I came up the shelf to eye-level with the reef to watch Matt's ascent. Matt, though, for some reason, wasn't surfacing straight away. I realized instead he was swimming to Jen and Paul to check their tanks, risking losing his air en route to them. Each of us had a spare regulator and line to the tank, which they could give to him if he ran dry, but Jen and Paul were a decent swim away, over a hundred, hundred-twenty feet off, still bottomed by the anchor line below the boat, ghosts at the edge of visibility. Apparently, it was all the farther the Frenchman would go. Matt checked his watch, swam fiercely, rapidly burning off his air in deep inhales. I wondered if he would run dry even before starting the ascent up the line. The fish were darting from him as he cut the water without any trace of that limp, and schooling again behind his slashing body. With the sea re-forming itself to his strokes, it was hard to consider how far he was from the others. They were motionless at the anchor line save for the Frenchman's sharp arm strokes battling the drift. There was very little drift, only a soft plume of sand off bottom from the Frenchman's strokes. I wondered if Claire was worried about her husband or embarrassed to be his wife. When Matt was within a few feet of them he only gave them two hard thumbs up, not having any time to run through hand signals to check tanks. I knew he had just run dry. Jen pulled the Frenchman's hand to follow and they started up the line. At twenty feet Matt had shaken lose his tank and dropped his weights. The tank now airless and heavy came down crashing between Jen and Paul, snapping a brain coral, stirring more sand. Matt would climb out barely winded, but if it had been the Frenchman or Claire alone or with each other it would have been disaster. I didn't even know how Jen would do suddenly without air up the entire line, or whether the Frenchman would have given her his spare regulator without a panic.

But then it was done and they were out and the quiet and weight of the water closed back over us. Claire and I were alone at the shelf, with no drift to fight. I let the BCD expel, take me down the shelf a little, but not too much because I wanted to dive later. Claire stayed slightly above me. She understood you didn't have to be swimming around the whole time on a dive, and I would ask to dive with her again. There was far less life on this side where the shelf fell away, the unknown depth always below. I could let myself gently fall.

Seventy-five feet, the dark rock, then only hints of the reef's reds and gold above, my breathing slowed, ribs tightened up. I trained the bubbles to once a minute, now less, let my limbs fall limp. My heart found a slow beat, felt the ocean lining shifting, sea floor quickening deep underneath, and the darkness. Eighty, eighty-five, I let myself go, safe from the narcosis if I kept it short. Ninety, one hundred, and I let the BCD allow me softly deeper to one hundred ten.

I was too deep now to stay for more than a minute. Claire was directly overhead and motionless up at sixty-five, above her a warm canal to the surface, the softer blues and a white circle of light. I still couldn't see bottom, but still could feel the unseen life in the stream of current below, all of it innocent of gravity and weight and their awkwardness. I was past the non-decompression diving limits, the pressure and the ocean wrapping me tightly, the breathing gone to nothing. It was, there, what I remember of deep sleep. It was the narcosis softly, I felt the soft nitrogen loosening my head. I wondered what the fisherman's old skiff up somewhere on the surface would look like from under, the oars feathering, then cutting down the water, moving only to the rhythm of his strokes, the heavy boat failing to glide in between strokes. And the above and the below were becoming the same.

I wanted, very suddenly, for the first time, very eagerly, to return to the surface.

I followed my bubbles up to Claire and tapped my watch for us to rise. We took a safety stop on the way up because I had been that deep. From out of the night underneath us, a shadow. It was the divemaster on a surge, swimming quickly for the top, breathing strongly on the fly, bubbles boiling off his tanks. He might have been another sixty below me, watching Claire and me the whole time. He was a lousy divemaster but a marvelous diver, and he had very hard lungs.

twelve. *the eel and the husband*

When Claire and I finally climbed on board, Matt was exhilarated. "Put my tank down as free," he was saying to Rainer's boy. The divemaster already was sitting up on the bow smoking. "Tanks with holes are generally free on principle, I think."

"Petey, where you been?" Jen had unzipped her wetsuit in the heat and was showing quite a bit, down to the droplets beading between her breasts.

"At the shelf."

"We didn't make it off the line," she said.

"I noticed." The Frenchman was up by Lawrence resting his eyes to avoid embarrassment. Lawrence was sunburned, asleep.

"Sorry about the hole in my tank pissing away our bet, Pete," Matt said.

"That's okay," I said. "You talk to him yet?"

Matt glanced up at the divemaster. "No, didn't mind the excitement really." He regarded the divemaster and the thin trail of cigarette smoke. "I probably should have broken his nose by now."

"We'd all have curses on us by now," Jen said.

"Let me see if I had a chance anyway," Matt said. He wiped my air gauge.

"What was the shelf like, Petey?"

"It was splendid," Claire said.

"How was it, Petey?"

"The middle of a dream."

"Christ," Matt said. "You used ten minutes of air."

"That's about right," I said. "Pull up the anchor," I told Rainer's boy.

"But the bet," he said.

"The bet is off," I told him. "Pull the anchor."

"I wish an umbilical had wrapped my neck at birth," Matt said.

"How'd you like running dry?" I asked.

"First time," he said. "At least you gave me some warning."

"That was wonderful, Petey, your warning the rest of us."

"The divemaster should have checked the tanks," I said.

"I ran dry about thirty feet from the line," Matt said.

"That soon?" I said. "I saw you loose your gear up the line at twenty."

"I took a mouthful," he said. "By twenty I was singing to myself."

"It was all so exciting," Claire said. She had slipped out of her wetsuit to sun herself topless. She had delicate collar bones and narrow hips.

"Petey," Jen said, "tell us about the shelf."

"We saw an eel," Claire said.

"Coral snake," Jen said. "We saw it, too. That's why your husband wouldn't let go of the line."

Claire went to tilt her head in the sun alone. The Frenchman was still pretending sleep.

"They'll kill you," Matt said, raising his voice for the Frenchman's benefit. "They hit you and you don't even make it out of the water."

"Petey, if I have to be paired with him the whole summer—"

"We'll pass him off," Matt said. "We'll have new people in, too, and we'll make them take him."

"Go easy," I said. "You might have been scared in the water once."

"Not *in* the water," Matt said. "Not for myself."

"Go easy then because he's French," Jen said.

"Why?" Matt asked.

"Because he's just found out his arrogance is without basis," she said.

Matt laughed, then carried on a false laugh long enough again to make sure everyone on the boat knew at whom he was laughing.

thirteen. *the chorus girl backstage*

On the way in, the water had calmed and Rainer's boy made good time. We had decided not to risk another dive that afternoon with the old tanks. The sky was high and overcast, but with many breaks. Jen laid her head asleep on Matt's shoulder and had peeled away most of her wetsuit to sun herself, now as topless as Claire. Matt was asleep and the Frenchman and Lawrence hadn't yet opened their eyes. The boat's wake splashed and hushed in my head. I sat next to Claire, remembering, watching the rhythms of Jen's breathing, slow and full.

"She doesn't like me," Claire said.

"Who?"

"The one whose bosom you are watching."

"Yes," I smiled.

"Why doesn't she like me?"

"Because your husband ruined her dive."

"I am embarrassed of him," she said.

"Don't be," I said. "It takes a few dives to be comfortable under water. Though you seem to be very comfortable already."

"She has wonderful breasts." Jen had a short scratch from her wetsuit zipper across her heart.

"Yes," I smiled, "I noticed that, too."

"Do you know the Folies-Bergère in Paris?"

"I know England much better than France," I said. "I know they say it was once spectacular, though."

"I have seen the pictures backstage with the chorus girls in them. They sit cross-legged before a giant mirror to smoke and the tapestry that separates them from the stage is behind them. It is quite a tapestry. Of old Seville, I think. Those chorus girls each has breasts like hers."

"I'll have to visit," I said.

"It is not like that anymore. Do you still love her?"

"Who?"

"Who. Who do you think who?"

The boat was bucking softly on the waves. Claire's neck and shoulders already were reddening in the sun. "You should cover your top," I said. "You're burning."

"And?" she asked.

"I used to," I said. "We went together at college, but that was twelve years ago."

"Do you still?"

"What?"

"Love her," she said.

"Who's to say?" I said.

"Does she love you?"

"Who's to say. I don't think of it."

"When I was a girl," she said, "I used to want very badly to be the chorus girl backstage at Folies-Bergère."

"You could have done it."

"It's not like that anymore backstage and I am too thin anyway."

"You're not," I said.

"I am. She is, too, really. It is only her breasts that resemble the chorus girls'. I have stared at them more than you."

"I don't know," I smiled, looking around to see if anyone else was awake yet.

"Where are you from?" she said.

"From all over," I said. "Like she is."

"Is that why you love her?"

"Maybe it's part of why I used to love her," I said.

"You are so careful," she said. The clouds had broken to sun and heat. "Where is all over?"

"Places in the States, then school north of Lancashire and then to London."

"You live in London now?"

"No," I said. "St. Simons Island."

"Is it Caribbean?"

"Coastal U.S."

"In the South?"

"Georgia is as South as it gets."

"With the redneckers?"

"No redneckers," I said. "Except for you, burning in this sun."

"You are afraid of me bare." She smiled and pretended to cover the freckles on her breasts modestly. Then she blushed at her own joke. The bloom in her chest spread up her throat to her face. She had very high cheekbones, reddening now, too.

"Why?" she asked.

"Why what?"

"Why do you still live there?"

"I don't know," I said. "I promised not to move."

"You promised who?"

"Her. And her father."

"I once told my father as a girl I wanted to work at the Folies-Bergère."

"Did he approve?"

"No, but he was sentimental. His father took him in there a back way as a boy in the thirties. As a boy he had seen the tapestry and the bare chorus girls smoking and swearing playfully at him."

"It's too bad you could not become a chorus girl, then."

"No," she said, wiggling her toes, "it is a miserable life. Just as any dream." She brushed a blond hair off her lips.

I went up front and took Lawrence's hat off his head. He was snoring.

"Your part," I said to her, "in your hair, is burning, too. You're too fair for this sky." The hat came down to her eyes. I sat down again beside her.

"I think that she loves you," she said, her breath on my shoulder.

The motor deepened with a tremor of passed thunder and Rainer's boy took us slowly into the close, protected Cay. The Cay smelled of hot shells and wet sand. It had rained there. The tide was out terribly and the boats were all landlocked. The boy followed the last green string of channel to the dock. He stood at the wheel caressing it and did not look back.

fourteen. *the .22*

We would use all new gear. We waited overnight for the tanks to arrive and finally worried that nobody had told Fitch to fly them in for us. The next morning I went with Jen to send Fitch to Freeport. It was uncommonly cool. The winds were coming off the sea from the north. We were supposed to dive very late that day, and Fitch might have time to return with the new gear before the dive. I showed Jen the wisteria-way path down to the airstrip. The stone was strewn with shards of broken glass.

"So who gets the Frenchman today, Petey?" Her chemise was sheer and teal, with a low neckline and a cut to the curve of her calf. It didn't match her eyes. The path dipped and I took her hand.

"I don't think he'll be back," I said.

"That would be too good."

"I saw him leave this morning on Fitch's first flight."

"I'm glad they're gone," she said. "Those two were bad luck."

"Only he left," I told her.

The slatestone path went to sand, and the breezes from the open dust runway came up, feathering her shift. I let go of her hand to pretend fishing for a cigarette.

"That other one," Jen said, "the other one has the eye for you, Petey. She's been watching."

"How so?"

"Petey, don't tell me you're not interested."

"Okay."

"Don't pretend, Petey. She was watching you the whole afternoon after we dove."

"Not as much as she was watching you."

Fitch was gone but the single-prop stood in the shade. We went to leave him instructions. On the cold white seat was a small and shiny black .22. Apparently Fitch had lost his sense of humor. Jen laughed when she saw the gun and said for us to fire off a few rounds. We looked around the seat for a pen but the whole seat was .22. I finally found a pen but gave it to Jen to write the instructions. With the .22 in the cab, the seat smelled like a burnt wick. Jen penned the note and we left quickly without speaking.

We took a different path back that would put us out at the terrace. The terrace was full of newcomers and a half-hearted breeze. The ocean was heaving quietly. We stood apart from the breakfast murmur and the morning heat began to come on. On the table in the center there were cut fruit and melons, smelling fresh and sweet. I wasn't hungry.

"Petey?"

"Let's go in," I said.

Matt sat with Lawrence at the table next to the bar. Lawrence was reading another old *Times*. "And where have you two been?" Matt asked.

"Making love," Jen said, and she blew me a kiss.

"Did you save me some?" Matt asked.

"We saved you all of it," I said. "We were leaving Fitch the instructions for new gear."

fifteen. *spilled lager and a fight*

That afternoon the restlessness was back. I went back to the room. I lay in a stretch cotton hammock out the glass door and the sun broke in and out of the clouds. The morning cool was long spent. I let myself sway to the hot winds up off the water and the memories that glowed like embers.

It was hours from night, but I let myself think about her. Though I knew I should not. I let my fingers drag on the planks underneath and I studied the white-stoned walls, two doors down, that hung cotton. I swayed in the shade, the stiffness in my ligaments from the dive only now beginning to work itself out, and I went with her many times again to the cozy pub where the two of us had spent afternoons together while we were in school. The place always smelled of spilled lager and a fight, with the owner and a few locals sitting crookedly on their crooked broken oak chairs. It was a small coastal town in the north of England which once devoted itself entirely to whaling, and there the locals loved to mix it up. Petey, punch a nobody for the hell of it, she used to giggle, let's see what happens. I thought once or twice she might try it herself. She had loved it there. The ocean breeze quit. The smoke from the cigarettes crept on the planks without lifting.

sixteen. *the virus*

"Look, Pete." It was Lawrence standing over the hammock. "There's something I wanted to say, but not in front of the others. I wanted to say it to you before, but I didn't know what to make of it."

"I didn't hear you come in the front," I said.

He sat on the planks. For a few moments he was winded and quite nervous.

"Do you want the hammock?" I asked. "I've had it all afternoon."

He was hot already in the straight sunlight. "No, it's all right, Pete. You're a friend, though."

"What is it then?"

"I've heard some things, Pete."

"Where?"

"On the boat, and I really feel we ought to go to Rainer."

"When on the boat?"

"After you and the others had gone in. I was fighting the waves and hoping for the drams to work."

"It was just Rainer's boy with you."

"And the divemaster," he said.

I sat up in the hammock and shook out the afternoon's thoughts. "The divemaster came back up while we were under?"

"About ten minutes in, I think. I was quite spent and feigning sleep, hoping the real thing would come on when he climbed up."

"How long was he up?"

"About five minutes."

"Five minutes out," I said.

"They're not supposed to do that, are they?" he asked.

"Never," I said. "I knew he'd left Matt but I figured he was always in somewhere watching us."

"He wasn't out long, only five minutes."

"Five minutes under water is plenty of time for your day to go wrong," I said.

"I suppose so," he said, "but that's not all of it."

"What else?"

"I didn't want to say in front of the others. I could hear Matt saying I was dreaming."

"What is it?"

"But I knew I could say it to you, Pete."

"You can."

His cheeks still had sun from the day before out on the boat. He might have had a nervous flush, but I couldn't tell.

"You can tell me," I said again. But I waited for him, because he hadn't told me last night and it must have overwhelmed him, whatever it was.

"Okay, Pete, here it is. They were speaking very quickly and in French. I don't know if they thought I was asleep or if the boy had forgotten I was speaking it to Paul earlier on the way out."

"You knew the dialect?"

"Enough of it. The boy spoke very formally in the European except for a few declensions so it was easy with him. The Cayenne dialect was much more difficult, though, and the divemaster spoke mostly in imperatives, like he was giving orders and running things. He was quite hard to understand. They understood each other very well, though."

"What did you pick up?"

"The divemaster was quite animated. He spoke about your virus."

I let my feet rest bare against the hot planks. The water would be warm for the dive later.

"What did he say?"

"He said the virus was spreading."

"He said so, did he?" The Obeah don't care about disease unless it affects their own.

"He said so, Pete. 'Spreading' or 'moving.' They were speaking very quickly and he with that dialect."

"I am going to ask you something, Lawrence, that I have to ask you, so please don't take offense."

"Okay, Pete."

"Were you dreaming it?"

"I wasn't dreaming it, Pete."

"You had at least four drams in you by then."

"It was more like six," he said. "I was quite desperate to sleep by then."

"Six drams would settle an elephant, Lawrence."

"Not this elephant, Pete."

"Six drams," I said.

"I didn't even fall asleep at all, Pete. I faked it the whole way back. Even when you were stealing my hat. I was afraid to give myself away."

"Cagey," I said.

"Scared," Lawrence said. "That Obeah. I'd hate to have him as an enemy."

"What else did they say?"

"A lot of business, really, the rest of it. Getting the boat in before the tide ran too low, and the boy asking if wasn't it more dangerous to dive low tide."

"It is," I said.

"The divemaster laughed at him," Lawrence said.

"He's a lousy divemaster."

"I think we should go to Rainer, Pete."

"Did he say anything else?" I asked.

"He said 'back to mother' before he went into the water again. What's that about, Pete?"

"Nothing I know of," I said.

"I'm going to discuss it with Rainer, Pete. If there's disease around, we should know about it, take some precautions."

He was slumping badly, a picture of drooping jowls. I handed him a bottle of Gilbey's that had found its way out under my hammock. It was near three by the sun and I had to figure it out before we went out on the boat that afternoon with them again.

"They had no idea you were awake?"

"No, Pete. They never knew. Did you know I was awake?"

"No," I said.

"I played it off even though I was about to be sick a couple of times, then the drams started up and I slept a little."

"You slept? You said you didn't sleep at all."

"Just for a couple of minutes, Pete. I woke up just as Matt came bursting out of the water."

"Did you dream any of this, Lawrence?"

"I swear I didn't, Pete. It was only a couple of minutes I slept."

The timing of it did fit. Out five minutes, then the divemaster would have time to swim away, then back under Claire and me at the shelf.

"I'm definitely going to have a talk with Rainer."

"Listen," I said. "Hold off. Wait until we get a little more information."

"Look, Pete, I don't do well with sickness. I'm not like you and the others. I tend to sweat a lot anyway."

"We won't wait too long, Lawrence, only until we know a little more."

"I don't know, Pete."

"Look, if we want Rainer to be straight with us, we've got to know what we're talking about."

"I guess, Pete."

"If you go to him now, you're liable to get flat denials and he'll only pass the word for everybody to clamp up."

"I guess you're right, Pete."

"And they're going to make damn sure nobody says a word around you."

"I don't want to be left out of it," he said.

"Right now, you're right in it," I said. "If you keep going out on the dives and pretending sleep, they're liable to talk about all sorts of things."

"That sounds right, Pete."

"You're the ears, Lawrence, unless you go talking to Rainer."

"I get it, Pete."

"It most likely is nothing," I said.

"I guess I could have heard it wrong through the dialect," he said.

"But if it is anything, then we'll need your ears on the boat."

"You really think it's nothing, Pete?"

"It's nothing," I said.

"I like going out with you on the dives anyway, Pete," he said.

"Just keep it quiet then."

His forehead was shiny. He was sitting with his mouth open. I hadn't had much of the gin because of the dive that afternoon, even a shallow dive. I didn't want DCS. The bottle was empty now only from Lawrence's relying on it. I felt certain he had the virus figured all wrong.

seventeen. *nights*

Several days passed. Then several more. Until Fitch flew the tanks in, we could only wait. There was always heavy dusk, then dark, hours until dawn. But I had long grown accustomed to these parts of the day. When time turned on itself.

There was a refuge of sorts for people like me. The Advena Maris had a bar for its midnight wanderers and often the two lights and dry air lured me in. It smelled like cancer and trespasses inside. There every night a kid from Kansas City was on bourbon talking to the bartender. The kid from Kansas City was nineteen, crew-cutted, and always very drunk. I never saw him in daylight. The bartender was an old Bahaman with wide eyes and a boy's face who sometimes spoke very formally. Everyone called him the Chief.

"Good Evening, Pete," he said to me. "How are your dives?"

"Imaginary," I said.

"Say," the kid said, "I'll bet you're glad Lila's back in town."

"I think I've heard this one," I said.

"He's gone to Kansas City again, Pete," the Chief said.

"I saw her this morning get off the four-twenty with three beat up bags and a Greek man," the kid said. "Everybody loves Lila."

"How's a gin, Pete?"

"Okay."

The others were always long asleep, long tired of the wait for new gear, or of drinking and heat. It was never good to drink the night before a dive and I often did anyway, not knowing if by morning Fitch would have flown in the new tanks. The closest decompression chamber was in Freeport and they wouldn't be able to fly me there because the altitude would only worsen it.

"Remember that giant green hat she wore on the windy days?" the kid said. "Show off, that Lila. That hat never even swayed in the wind. That's Lila for you, defying mother nature."

These nights often there was another of the resort's guests sitting alone at a table out on the terrace by a candle flickering. It might be a tourist near the end of his stay, or Fitch drinking between flights or straight through the night. If it was a tourist he would keep to himself and his drink and wonder what he was going back to. If it was Fitch he would hold his warm drink in both hands and try to think of nothing, dipping his red head slowly until sleep took him.

"Say," the kid said, "Lila sure looked great getting off that train wearing nothing but the yellow dress with nothing but Lila underneath."

"Hey, kid, shut up," Fitch said, and the red head would begin to nod again.

"That Greek fella was watching his back the whole time. He must be seeing her nowadays," the kid said.

"Here's a drink there, Kansas." The Chief kept him full.

"It's impossible dating Lila," the kid said. "She breaks a heart every time they break a seal on a new bottle of Gilbey's. Everybody loves Lila."

"Everybody loves Lila," Fitch said. "It's a whale of a story, kid. Shut up."

When Fitch was flying us in the month before, he hadn't yet had the close call he now wouldn't talk about. Then, he was still doing his stunts in the old single-prop. Jen and I had locked eyes once after he had cut the engine for a moment. The Chief always brought Fitch dry gins in matching thick antique glasses that Fitch hated.

"I don't do them anymore," Fitch said again to me one night at the bar. We were both smoking out on the terrace on tiles crawling with brown centipedes. The tiles were slick, wet from a shower.

"The stunts," I said.

"Yeah, those stunts. I don't want to talk about it."

"I know."

"It was a hell of a thing to do anyway," Fitch said.

"I know."

"You want to hear the story, Mr. Cole?"

"Okay," I said. I supposed he'd rather tell it now than explain what he'd been doing all this time instead of flying in our new gear.

"Well, I'm not telling it, Mr. Cole. 'Cause why?"

"'Cause it's personal," I mumbled.

"You're goddamned right it's personal having the Christ scared off you."

The Chief was clinking glass bottles inside behind the bar and the kid wore a wide smile on his face as if he were listening, though we knew he was still in Kansas City.

"You know, personal," Fitch said. "Like when you were making eyes at your buddy's girl on the flight in."

After Jen and I had caught a stare, I had settled back in the seat under the plane's hum once I knew we were straight. I had expected the vertical dips and falls, but not the single-prop's lateral wagging. A cracked window had kept cold air on my face. I had watched the green and blue swirls off the sand bars below, the chloasma-brown jetties, felt attached to nothing when the plane spun slightly on even keel.

"Maybe you've had a few extras tonight," I said to Fitch.

"That's an easy one, Mr. Cole. But we both know I'm right anyway." The liquor was always hot and sometimes stale. As the days went the Advena Maris overfilled with tourists and Fitch quit coming around, and those nights so late up in the bar it was only the occasional tourist with a beer who would talk to no one.

"Say," Kansas City would call to the tired drinker out on the terrace, "say, did you ever see Lila get steamed good?"

The tourist knew he was rambling by the nod given by the Chief. We had all heard the stories and we all listened to them again. There was nothing to do to set the kid quiet.

"I loved her when she was mad down at Henri's drinking Gilbey's," the kid said. "I'd hide her drinks and pay her tab and she'd get so damned steamed. Say, I loved to steam her off. One night we were going back to the flat and I knocked her green hat away. Lila said something about a gentleman and a prince and broke my nose. Say, I used to love to see Lila mad."

When I went to the bar these nights I always sat under the warm lamp that lit a small spotlight of floor at my foot and brought me out of the dark. None of the others ever sat in the old chair by the lamp, preferring the weak candles and the breeze up the terrace walls and the centipedes on the tiles outside. The old floor was dark oak brought in polished from the States. The light bounced away from my foot. You were sitting on a cloud some nights, depending upon how well-stocked the Chief kept you. He was almost always ahead of us and I surely would have had decompression sickness if we had been diving during the days, and if I hadn't eventually held him off.

"I've plenty," I said to him once, feeling the chair softening, turning to thunderhead.

"That's why they call him the Chief," the kid said. "Say, I could use a bourbon, though."

"Your glass is full," the Chief said to him. He returned behind the bar and began drying the old heavy glasses that Fitch hated.

"Well, we all know the pattern," the kid said. "Lila runs off with one and comes back with another. She'll have him shave and wash up for a late dinner at Seran's soon as they're back and while he's in the tub she'll be slapping backs and saying hey boys at the hotel bar. Everybody loves buying Lila drinks, but nobody could steam her off like I could. Sure, she's been away longer this time and come back with a ring, but in an hour or two she'll have the green hat up and the gin'll be flowing."

"He's gone back again, Pete."

"I suppose you've got to let him go, Chief."

"Oh, yes, you have to let him go."

There were always these nights. In the days we all were waiting on the beaches together for the dives to start again, except, that is, for Claire. She preferred to be alone, now that her husband had gone. In the mornings just before dawn I sometimes watched her fishing from shore in the cove. She cast and drew the line through the dark water, a pool of ink, and she cast again, arching her back and stepping as she cast, the rod gently bending to the test, her body a graceful whip. She wore to her thighs a white blouse which shimmered when the line hit the water. We never spoke. I'd watch from the dock until dawn rose and streaked veins in the sea, chasing the last pretense of cover. That was how the days always started. But there were always these nights.

"You might wonder what's under the green hat," the kid said. "Come on, we all did, and I was the only one got to see, really see, you know, when it came off unexpected. I'll tell you what I saw. It was naked Lila. I got to see it for a minute. Sure, we all got to see Lila without her dress on and the green hat carefully propped beside the bed. Boy she had the curves and the heat. Even standing in a room fully clothed and with her bare I felt like she was the one dressed. You know what I mean. That's Lila."

"Chief?"

"On the way, Pete."

"But knock the green hat off her, see that matted blond hair and the stun in her eyes and she ain't got a stitch on all of a sudden. Even standing over me on the sidewalk helping me back to my feet and saying sorry Ernie, about the bloody nose, and me saying forget it, Lila, she was bare to the wind. Here's your hat, Lila. Ernie, get me a car, I'm going around the park."

I spent the daytime with the others, watching Jen snorkeling in her green wetsuit with the zipper slightly open at the neck, and watching Lawrence watch the two of us to see when we'd catch eyes, and Matt uncaring about it all. She and I used to snorkel away whole vacations, spending sun-burnt days with only our heads under water, our minds drifting with arms of seaweed, tasting the salt on our lips. And Matthew still uncaring about it all.

Another very late night I came into the bar and there was a man in the chair by the lamp, spotlighted very old and feebled, his cheeks having long sunk and his eyes recessed but still bright. He wore an evening jacket left on from the dinner. There was a wood stove lit by the fireplace that dried out the salt air and only made it slightly hotter but less uncomfortable than the humid terrace with its centipedes. The candles wobbled. I did not want to sit out there.

"Should we play poker?" he asked me.

"We should," I said. "Are you from Derbyshire?"

"Devon," he said.

"We have a Brit in our party," I said. "Matthew Hawkes."

"Don't bring him up here now. It is a very hard existence, being British. We will have to examine one another's speech to determine who is wealthier."

"He's fast asleep," I said.

"You, for instance, have spent some time there."

"Four years at Hatry College."

"I teach at Walcott. But you are not originally from England."

"The States."

"You see," he said, "I now am exhausted."

We went to the terrace to the only lit table and the wet air.

"Should I ask the bartender for a deck?" I said.

"I've my own cards," he said.

"Would you like my money now?" I asked.

"You may count the cards," he said, "or ask for your own deck."

"Gentlemen's rules," I said. The Chief came with our drinks. I told him we wouldn't need cards.

The Professor's cards were worn and slack in the wet air. The centipedes were crawling over the railing and dropping into the dark wisteria tangles below. Our candle flames were in danger of falling still.

"What are you professor of?" I asked.

"Anthropology," the Professor said. He shuffled and the old hands shortly would separate me from my money.

"Say," Ernie from K.C. called, "I bet you're glad Lila is back in town." From the terrace you could see him when he slumped into the light behind the Chief's bar.

"He thinks he's in Kansas City," I said.

"Very interesting," the Professor said. "He is a very interesting one, this Kansas City fellow. I have been listening to him all night."

"Yes, he plays here all the time."

"It's right up my road, really," he said.

"Ernie from Kansas City?"

"Yes, Ernie."

"What do you study, Professor?"

He listened for a moment for the surf, but it was silent this night. "Anxiety of self-dissolution and its rituals," he said.

He dealt to himself marvelously and won the hand easily. We noticed the new stars and the air cooling, but still wet.

"Say, did you ever get Lila to play you poker?" the kid said to no one. "She played poker like those guys out on the porch are. She'd get you to play strip, remember, and turn the bar into naked jaybirds in ten minutes."

"I don't see it," I said to the Professor. He dealt again and I felt the luck changing when he offered to open the bet at one hundred.

"She, this Lila, seems to be his distraction," the Professor said.

"From what?"

"Dealer takes none. From the end."

"That's a little more direct than we tend to be around here," I said. "Four, please."

The Chief brought us new drinks. The very old Professor had three queens and two two's.

"May I ask you," he said, "and forgive me, this is my area of study, though I know it makes others quite uncomfortable, may I ask you, and tell me, please, if I may not, may I ask why you have come south of Exuma Cays?"

"Of course," I said. "For the dives."

"Oh, a marvelous distraction," he said, a smile baring, warming his face. "There are so many to choose, but diving is indeed one of the best."

"Say, you can't cheat without a shirt," Kansas City yelled out to us. "It was the first thing she'd win off you. Damn that Lila, bringing her own cards."

I went for my wallet.

"Old Ernie's distraction seems an urgent business," I said to the Professor.

The Professor simply looked at me and began to deal. We each bet 300 on the hand to be called as it was dealt upturned.

"One pair of fives, one nine, and one ace," he said.

"Two pair, sevens and fours, king high," I said. With this 300 pounds I would be getting back toward even.

"Three fives," the Professor dealt himself. I gave him the money.

He was a marvelous card player who refused to cheat. He surely counted played cards and could remember a shuffle, but if he was smart enough to remember, then he deserved to win anyway. He helped to pass the damp night. It was painless losing to him, though I would have to wire new money.

"I am not convinced," I told him in the middle of a seven-card, "of your hypothesis."

"Say," Ernie from K.C. yelled again, "did you fellas know Alan Watt? He got Lila naked once switching decks. Did you hear how it ended? Lila sitting there in nothing but a string of pearls and leaning way out over the table saying, say Al, keep dealing, let's see if you can't lose some, too. And Al saying, sure Lila, and what's in it for me, and Lila saying, well Al, how about me and right here on this table right now."

"It is no hypothesis," the Professor said. "It is well-researched that anxiety of one's end dictates one's actions. We are only a collection of rituals for diversion, but we must allow it."

"Why allow it?"

"Without—" the Professor began. A breeze kicked at the pound notes on his side of the old table and he lost his thought. He rested his thin wrists on the notes lightly, with a gentleman's casualness that did not emphasize that he had won them from me. He might have been listening for the waves to break again.

"Have you ever had the narcosis?" he asked me.

"You know of the narcosis?"

"From nitrogen," he said, "in the blood."

"Yes, it loosens your head. It's very dangerous," I said.

"Have you had it?"

"Twice," I said. "I misread a divechart once. Once I went deeper to feel it anyway."

"Is it beautiful?" the Professor asked. "I have heard that it is beautiful."

"It can kill you," I said.

"Is it beautiful?"

"Yes, but it's no way to dive."

"Diversions are identity," the Professor said, remembering the lost thought.

I was looking for the cigarettes.

"Say," the kid called from inside again, "say, don't you know Al Watt couldn't lose to get naked with that stacked deck he brought until it occurred to him to just start folding full houses and trey aces, until finally in his briefs it occurs to Al he ain't got it in him, you know, the deed with Lila, if he loses one more. Say, don't you know Lila knew she had him then. Al Watt went to the bar for a shooter and courage and came back looking to win instead. He had the cards for it if he'd quit folding. He'd make it a matter of pride just keeping Lila there naked. Say, that Lila is a cool one. Ernie, get me the green hat. Sure, Lila. She beat Al Watt four kings he'd folded the hand before to a full house. She'd swiped up the cards and hid them in an armpit when everybody had watched Al take his shots with the barkeep. Poor Al, never saw anybody leave a bar like that, all naked and pure droop. I loved Lila."

"Do we suppose that Ernie from Kansas City is mad?" the Professor asked.

"He's only soused."

"Only soused?"

"Soused and only slightly mad," I said.

"Could you get that bartender?" the Professor said.

"Chief?" I called.

The Professor dealt several more fine hands, one of which I won. The breeze went its coolest before dawn, but the air was still dark, thick again, and there was no hint of a new day's light, only a black sheet of night. He was a wonderful card player with a mathematician's brain and an anthropologist's sense of when I was full of it. He knew many games. We had little need to speak for long stretches of the night. The candle once went out and the air held the scent of a fired gun. The Chief barely relit the wick with a cigarette he was smoking.

"So what is your chosen distraction?" I said to the Professor, when the flame was safely back up.

"I have many," he said. "Cards, traveling, Laphroaig and a few other single-malts."

Inside the kid was pantomiming the Chief drawing off old liquor. "Don't forget scholarly detachment," I said, "from the Beast herself."

"Oh, yes," he said, "my most wonderful diversion." He lay down his cards, faces to the table. "Through academic study of Her, I allow myself the conceit of knowing the truth."

"Beautiful," I said.

"Yes," he said, "I suppose it is." He had left out his cigarettes and they were damp.

This made him smile. I gave him one of mine.

"Say," the kid from Kansas City called out to us again, "say, I'll bet you're glad Lila is back in town."

"Shut up, soaker." It was Fitch in a cold shadow, and we couldn't tell how long he'd been in there that night, or how many nights he'd been there, in the shadows, inside. "Shut up, you soaker," Fitch said again. "These men are trying to distract each other."

"Say," the kid said, "say do I wonder what happened between us, after the kisses and caressing and the wrestling in our flat, and the walks in moon and the salt on her lips and those soft strokes of tongue she put on your ear."

"Shut up," Fitch said, "you damn soaker."

"I could've cared less about the ages," the kid said, "she was older, who cared, she was old Lila. The days she was gone and the green hat stayed behind. Hey, Lila, I say to the hat, how about a hand of rummy. Say, Lila could put the burn back in you. She wasn't not sleeping out sometimes, but the green hat stayed with me except on those marvelous windy days when I couldn't be without her."

The Chief came over once more and the Professor and I refused him. The Professor had been buying my drinks for an hour on courtesy.

"Did you know Fitch was in there?" I said to the Chief.

"Of course, Pete. He's his own bottle." The Chief stayed with us on the terrace, leaning against the damp wall.

"Well, I'm wondering," Fitch said from the dark, "what makes diving such a wonderful ritual, Doc."

The Professor was folding my IOUs neatly. "It has the appropriate elements of risk, beauty, and control," he said, "as well as lack of control, and fear. I suppose you must become accustomed to the water, do you not, yet you must fear it to remain of a safe mind, and once you return to the top, there is a sense of a mastery of nature."

If Fitch found gear by the next week, we already had booked a dive with twelve-foot tigers. It was a tame shark in these waters and wasn't supposed to hit divers, but sometimes did. Yet I wanted to go in to see her because she was older than man by ninety million years. Her eyes were bead black. I wanted to feel her cold skin and stay in the water with her, because she'd outlast any dream, or any nightmare, she was a piece of the sea.

"I'll be goddamned if I tell the story," Fitch said. "Goddamn knocked the Christ right out of me. Probably a good thing, though, huh, Doc, losing your religion at four thousand feet?"

"A distraction," the Professor said.

"What?" said Fitch.

"Religion," said the Professor.

"Right, good riddance," said Fitch.

"And losing your religion."

"What?"

"A distraction, too," the Professor said.

"Well, I'm still not telling the story," Fitch said. "I'll be goddamned to sound like some soaker."

"Say, Lila," the kid called again, "say, Lila, I said when she got off the train today with the Greek guy. Hey, Lila, it's been three years. Hey, Lila, where you been? What happened to Pascal the French salesman you left with? We all knew he was a goner."

"Say, shut up, soaker," Fitch said.

"You've got to let him go there," I said.

"Oh, yes, Pete, you've got to," the Chief said. We had forgotten he was standing behind us on the newly dried terrace. He had refilled our drinks again. He left for the bar.

"Say, Lila, I shout, how about a trip to the track or some shooters downstairs? They got new stools at Henri's and a porch in the breeze now. God, it's good to have her back."

"You're going to the giggle farm," Fitch said from the shadows, "you damn soaker."

"But Lila didn't hear me, of course, for the wind whipping up across the tracks, through the station, over the crowd and the new trains going out and one very distant one coming in or stalled on the tracks, how would you know?"

"See you at the giggle farm," Fitch said.

The cards with the Professor obviously now were over. It was time for dawn but there seemed no threat of light. The breezes had changed and would be whipping down the rock, standing up the waves, but the tide seemed always coming in, though there were only terrace candles and the lamps inside. The terrace railing now had become the last edge of sight.

"Hey, Lila, I shouted anyway across the tracks, and it hits me she would have heard me if she had her green hat on. Say, Lila? But the wind, the wind, and no green hat. Say. The blond hair fussing in the breeze and the Greek putting a giant hand on her shoulder and Lila looking up at him. Say."

"Say," Fitch said, "would anybody mind if that goddamned soaker shut the hell up?"

"Lila was naked in the yellow dress without the hat, out there for all the world in trains to see, and it wasn't any kind of deal to her. Say, Lila, I whispered and Lila looked my way. Sure, I was lost in the crowd and the breeze. Say. Those green hat days. They must be over."

"Thank god," Fitch said. "Now shut up."

Some nights this late you could hear the surf or the air rustling the palms or dead quiet centipedes dropping to the wisteria, and smell the salt long after if you went from the terrace to sit inside, or feel the stars shimmering through you, even taste the long dewless blades of grass—there was never any dew—while waiting for the dawn. But not this night. Kansas City laid his head on the dark bar, Fitch faded back into the shadows, the dives and everything else were memory.

"Thank you for the games," the Professor said. He stood up on uncertain feet. He had been calmly silent through the end of the kid's ramblings. He was a man who should be tired of the night but still couldn't bear to sleep through it.

"It was a privilege losing to you," I said. "I apologize for providing no challenge."

"Not at all," he said. "Are you sleeping, too?"

"In a few minutes," I said.

"Good, then, Pete. If I don't see you here first, I'll see you on the water."

"On the water?"

"For the shark dive," he said. "Next week. Why do you think I am here?"

"I heard we had another for that dive," I said, laughing at his secrecy. "I should have figured you to be him."

"My age prejudiced you," he said. He smiled as though his age were a joke on me, and made a toast of his last glass with its lone ice cube. "To the narcosis."

"To Ernie from Kansas City," I said.

"Yes," he said, "of course, to Ernie, too."

He worked with a cane down to the terrace steps. I helped him by a thin arm and his wrists shook, but the water would take care of this. A man on ground isn't the same man in the water.

"Have we a good divemaster?" he asked.

"Not at all," I said.

He stopped to look at me, the worry traveling his blue eyes. He regained himself.

"Well," he said. "No matter. The sharks will probably finish us off before we can take this divemaster's word for some minor miscalculation."

"Yes," I said.

"The ocean's antibodies," he was chuckling as he went down the steps.

"Good night, Professor," I called to him.

"Good night, Pete. And get some sleep." He left and I stood alone then at the terrace wall.

I lit a cigarette and a new touchless memory. The cigarette was dry and sweet. It was the last of the executioners that Jen had given me. Inside, the Chief was refilling bottles quietly in the dim light behind his bar, and the silhouette of the kid asleep, head on bar. There still was no sign of dawn. The memory and the smoke drifted into black, caressed empty air, touched no one, went.

eighteen. *the conspiracy of the tides*

At a quarter of eight that next morning I went to Rainer's office to phone Dobbs to check on my theatres and to have money sent. The sprinklers were clicking and bringing false rain, making it feel earlier in the season than it was. The blades of grass were dull and thick, but the garden roses were rigid as toothpicks. Inside, in the office, the new gear was set up. Fitch must have flown it in very late, or very early. It was the same thing.

Rainer wasn't yet at his desk checking in any new tourists. I called Dobbs and asked how things ran with the theatres. Fine, Dobbs said, not to worry. Did he need anything? No, Dobbs said, everything was handled. I said to let me know if he needed anything. Dobbs said he never did.

By luck down on the dock, the fisherman called Eduardo was tying off his skiff again. The waters were green and dead and had not yet lit; a stretch of thunderheads was clearing east and the sun still had yet to burn out of them. A crescent of moon balanced on the thin air, but the stars had gone in.

"Hello, fisherman," I waved to him.

"Hello, not-a-fisherman," he called back.

He had no fish in the boat or in the basins on the dock. The basins were white and empty even of water. His cheeks were shallow and unshaven. I tied off one of his lines in a hitch, smelled only the planks rotting on his skiff. The fibers from the wet sisal rope rent my fingertips, but wouldn't have cut his callused hands. The baling stitches on his forearms had burnt to bright red one clear day out.

"English cigarettes?" he asked me.

I handed him one and lit it. "Would you breakfast with me, Eduardo?"

"Oh, breakfast," he said. "I never eat it."

"How long since a meal?"

"Long enough," he said. His accent was tripping the English. He was very tired. "Is always long enough between meals," he said. "Even, I suppose, when they come every three hours on the clock."

"We're soft, if that's what you mean," I said.

"I only come in for water," he said. He drew shortly on the cigarette. "I mean nothing about softness."

"Why have you loaded the empty basins on the dock?" I asked.

He looked back out on the thunderheads breaking and the first hard sun. "I don't know," he turned to me, "habits."

"I heard you had a marvelous catch a time back."

"I must have caught them nearly all."

"When the winds turn around you'll catch the rest," I said.

This made him smile yellow teeth and straighten himself. "Yes, yes," he said, "there's always a spell for a few weeks like this in summer for no reason, pero is never forever. I never remember it until it passes and the fish are jumping into the basins again."

"How long do you go out today?" I asked.

"Until a good catch."

"Will you take me out with you?"

"Oh, Americans in the boat. She sinks."

"I can swim," I said.

"Yes, I remember," he said. "You are the one who likes to swim with the fishes I eat."

"The skipjack you gave to me was very good."

"I have only one cushion and I must sit on it."

"I'll split the strokes with you."

"You row?"

"Of course," I said.

"I must sit on the cushion," he said.

"I've a fifth of something or other in my room."

"Is it liquor?" he joked.

"Yes."

"Bring it."

"Where are we going?" I asked.

"Out to the conspiracy of the tides," he said.

"Yes, yes, Eduardo, can you be more specific?"

"A hidden coral, six miles due southeast."

"I'll get the bottle," I said.

"And some water," he said.

Back on beach, the black rock to the path was burning in the sun up to the treeline.

"And Peter Cole," he called.

"Yes?"

"Hurry, the tide is to turn and we can ride it out."

"Okay."

"And Peter Cole."

"Yes?" I said.

"More English cigarettes."

nineteen. *the ocean Mary*

The tide took Eduardo and me out slowly. We ate apples I took from the terrace. "These are very good," he said, "for something that does not swim."

"They float," I said.

"I have heard that about apples." He sat on the center plank with the oar handles resting on his lap. I sat in the shallow stern, which would take water with any swells, but the ocean was only a green pond.

"Throw them to the sharks," he said. I threw the cores out.

"Apples," he said. "Apples are muy."

"Muy what?"

"Muy everything today."

Without a breeze it would be hot by mid-morning. The tide soon began carrying us swiftly and the shore became only white glare.

"Tell me about the virus, Eduardo."

"Oh, the virus. Cigarettes for information?"

"It's not like that."

"Not many Americans want to sink with me."

"I'm a romantic."

"I do not think so."

"No."

"Then why are you here, Peter Cole?"

"Fighting the conspiracy of the tides," I said.

"They are no joke. Everyday, in and out, and still people do not believe in conspiracies. They kept me for forty-one years."

"I suppose sunset and sunrise are conspiracies, too?"

"Now, you are being silly," he said. He lit a new cigarette and smiled again. "She's a big joke to you," he said.

"Who?"

"The ocean Mary."

"No," I said.

"Without this ocean we only rest on a great chasm."

"And without these cigarettes we rest only on a great chasm."

"Yes," he said. "They remind you, and then kill you, too. After they gut you. To make sure that you heard them."

"You are a philosopher."

"Not me. You."

We were moving quickly without wind and oar. The sun began warming the boat planks and my forearms.

"When do we let out the nets?" I said.

"When we are ready to catch fish," he said. "Are you seasick already? I saw a wave yesterday."

"I'm not seasick."

"Do you talk to the fishes, Peter Cole, when you are down swimming with them?"

"I admire them," I said.

"Do they admire you?"

"I doubt it."

"They admire me," he said, "because I catch them, and then I eat them."

"Have you ever caught the virus?" I asked.

He began slowly arcing the oars, rowing air, then quit. "Damn on the virus," he said.

"It isn't disease, is it?"

We had slowed suddenly and rested deadly on a green sheet. He was watching dolphin jump a half mile east, the oar handles now cradled again in his lap.

"I'm sorry," I said. "I won't mention it again."

"Will you row?"

I took the oars and he kept his cushion to sit facing me in the stern, still watching the splashless grey forms playing away from us.

"Peter Cole," he said, "yes, I have had the virus."

I dug the rough oars into the water and began pulling us through. The sun now was high enough to heat the back of my neck and the water burned my eyes.

"I have had the virus, but now I am a fisherman. I leave code language to boys. I am a man, and I am only a fisherman."

My back tightened to the strokes and the heat. I watched the
skiff's short wake trailing.

"Is '*virus*' local for '*trade*'?" I asked him. "An organization of
trade?"

"Yes," he said.

"Smuggling?"

"Yes."

"Of what?"

"Oh, it is nothing, a little syndicate of boys on Fernandina.
A little capitalism of mostly narcotics and a gun or two. It changes
with the season. I was very hungry then. Now I would rather fast
for a month than have the virus again."

He rubbed the red baling stitch scars on his forearms and
closed his eyes.

"The measure of a man is not what he has been anyway," he
said, "but what he is today. Measures of old feats lead to status,
and I am against all status. I am against all things of order."

"Everything? Law?"

"I need none. I fish. Right now I am going to sleep."

"Tell me then, Eduardo, before you sleep—what are you for?"

He opened his eyes, green water. "Anarqìa," he said, pointing
at the white horizon. "And the fish," he said, "and not to swim
with. But to eat."

"You're an anarchist, Eduardo?"

"A very good one and a very sleepy one," he said. "Row like
that for an hour and wake me up."

twenty. *anarqìa*

I waited for the sun to move over top of the fisherman to wake
him. The heat was falling hard. I watched him sleep. He lay with
his back to the hot planks, his feet hanging over starboard and
drawing trails in the water. His chest was shallow, tanned darkly

and red where the ribs showed, falling gently to the rhythms of the oar strokes. I rowed through a breeze into stillness again, through a bed of rotting seaweed that lay like caul on the water, infected, stale in the air, then into clean salt breaths again. I was burning the back of my neck badly above the collar and knotting the muscles through my shoulders with each stroke, but I matched the rowing to his breathing and the hour went quickly.

"Eduardo," I said.

"He is asleep," he said, his eyes pinched shut.

"Tell him it's been an hour."

"He says he still has one quarter of the hour to sleep."

"Tell him to look at the sun."

He blinked his eyes wearily at the high white sky. "He says thank you for waking him."

"He's welcome."

He sat upright in the stern and rubbed his neck and head. "You rowed like this the whole hour?"

"Without a break."

"How are your hands?"

I showed him the blisters bubbling under the skin.

"Well, don't row anymore," he said. "We take a rest."

"I think you just took a rest."

"What rest? Who can sleep with Americans driving the boat?"

I took a handful of saltwater and rinsed my face of the sweat and heat. The blisters hadn't broken yet and the saltwater only cooled them. The breezeless water, with the sun straight over, the ocean was the same white haze burning off each way and ached behind my eyes.

"Are you with the anarqìa?" he asked me.

"No," I said.

"What is so dear that you can not let go of the system? Is it money?"

"I have some."

"And you cannot bear to part with it."

"I don't think I'd mind."

"Then, what can you not leave? You have power? Fame? Misery? Are you attached to your misery?"

"You sound like a psychiatrist."

"Who?" he asked.

"A headshrinker," I said.

"A cannibal?"

"Slightly different," I said.

"What is this thing that you cannot bear to lose in the system? It is all virus, you know."

"I'm not particularly attached to anything," I said.

"Ah, yes," he laughed. "The virus has infected you."

"What virus? I'm not with those smugglers on the Island."

"You know," he said. "The virus of capitalism and possession."

"If you define 'virus' so broadly, I suppose I'm infected. Who isn't?"

"I am not. I am attached to no thing," he said.

"Nor am I, really."

"Yes, you said that. But I am attached to no one as well."

We had been drifting for some time in meandering breeze. I had lost all sense of shore.

"And aha!" he said.

"What?"

"You cannot say the same, can you? Someone from what you perceive as your class has thefted your eye."

"Who wants to be attached to no one?" I asked.

"I do," he said. "True anarqìa breaks all constraints of emotion. Emotion leads to ties. Ties lead to structures. Structures lead to possession and perpetuation of the system."

"Who taught you this, Eduardo?"

"A seamstress from Russia named Ilse. Jesus and Mary I loved her. Oh, for some time she was 'the one who didn't get away,' as they say. She taught me to quit the communions in San Cristòbal. Juan Diego and The Lady. You could have no time for God with Ilse around." He stared at the sky's empty blue, smiling.

"Seems you are attached to her," I said.

"Oh," he said, "she died during the Revolution. She was too Left even for Fidel. I like to pretend never to have known of him."

"I'm sorry."

"Cord binding the soul," he said. "I was quite fortunate, though. I never would learn the anarqìa properly if it were not for Ilse. I used to gasp at her figure, but for a long time she would have nothing between us. She never wore clothes in her apartment because clothes were the creations of men to show difference between them where there is no difference. Clothes make classes."

"But you said she was a seamstress. It doesn't quite fit."

"Sì, she was very confusing."

"You had the virus."

"A little, but it went. You have it now."

"I believe that you still have it, old friend."

"I? The sun has melted your head. I am immune now."

"You like this boat, don't you?" I asked. "You possess this boat."

He leaned forward, smiling a crooked grin, looking around at the sunlight dancing on water. He cupped his hands to the water and splashed his face, seemed to startle himself.

"Sì," he said. "Okay, sì, I like the boat. The boat and I, we hop for forty years isle to isle together. The Archipelago de Sabana, the Archipelago de Camaguey, to another time, the soft current of Old Bahama Channel and the Windward Passage, to a time for

Câp Haitien, for one night only, a time for Mouchair Passage and back Silver Bank Passage to Mona Passage—I know these passages!—to Isla Mona, Vieques, Culebra, Tortola, Anguilla. A time for Nevis and Montserrat, Grande Torre and Pointe-à-Pitre, and Roseau. A time for Martinique Passage—another passage!—and Aves Ridge, a time for the Venezuelan Basin, a time for the entire Caribbean Outer Ring. I know the worker who toils in the water. I see the world is a whirlpool without edges, one long kidnapping. I see the ocean and sky blink as one. I see this boat belongs to no one. She belongs to the sea."

He stood in the boat, found his bearings on markerless water. "Ah, no wonder nobody likes talking to me," he said. "Put out the nets. We are here."

We only heard the fish at first, the dull thudding against the wood of the boat, as if it were the boat itself killing them. Then we saw them bobbing around us, bloated, belly up, smelling in the sun.

twenty-one. *the open ring reef*

Later we each had decided to freedive, except for Claire who would use a tank, because we were only diving to twenty-five. We took one of the new tanks and tested it ourselves in the water by the dock at Rum Cay. In the afternoon heat, sweat darkened her hairline and sparkled on her cheeks. She had taken off her wedding ring. The skin was flaking where she'd worn it, as if it still chafed her.

Jen had noticed the ring was gone, too. "It is so simple to be French," she whispered to me as we boated out of the Cay.

Rainer's boy stood steady-shouldered and took us not out into the sound but kept within a mile of the bending casuarinas and white shore. Claire sat next to me by the sitting steps and held her naked finger. The waves were nothing today. Lawrence was fidgeting under the false cabin with no Frenchman to talk to and unsure when to fall asleep. He might have to act a little with the water so calm out or taking drams would seem ridiculous.

"Do you think 'Happy' will stay in with us today?" Matt asked. The divemaster rode alone on the bow again and had spoken to no one.

"Don't provoke him," Jen said.

"I don't understand how he stays so wonderful," Matt said.

"He's a conversationalist," I said.

We anchored within two hundred yards of beach and from the boat were close enough to see the sisal on shore. The sands this south were barbeque red. The jetties went black into the water. The water was clear to the reef below and the sea turtles were stretching to move around the red coral. I helped Claire in and avoided her eyes. They were wide and brown. The rest of us went in after Claire went down. The divemaster never moved from the bow.

I held Jen's hand and we swam in without tanks. We were in with the sea turtles and the amazon greens and the coral that would burn your skin if you touched it. It was a small open ring reef. The sea turtles moved slowly and without us, unafraid of our touch. Claire had found a calm place off the coral, gently moving her fists in small circles. We were shallow enough that it stayed very bright.

As soon as Jen and I were settled down in the warmth she shook loose my grip to go up for air, slicing toward surface in the yellow bikini. Matt settled in beside me and wanted to play. It was a game we always played, he and I staring into each other until one of us had to go up for air. It was never me, of course, who had to go up first. He lasted a couple of minutes and surfaced and came down with Jen again. With our game, we forgot about Claire for awhile, but she was quite content breathing streams of soft bubbles off her regulator in the calm, floating off the coral without her husband. The coral red stayed in our eyes when we shut them. Jen went back up for air, then Matt. I went up for the first time when they surfaced the time after.

I used to freedive all day. There was nothing to go wrong when you freedove. There was no tank to empty, no regulator to loosen from your jaw, no chance for water in your lungs unless you opened your mouth and decided to swallow the saltwater. I settled a little off the bright coral, feeling a faint pulse off the floor moving through me to the surface. You would have to decide to put your head back and swallow hard, and open your throat.

We all went down and up again a few times, Jen then Matt, then Jen again, then Matt again, then me. It was the first time I had gone under partnering with Jen in some time and she took several trips up for breath, but it was as if she belonged down below while she was gone, and when down again it was as though she belonged on the surface, and out, and down below all at the same time again. She was surfacing at the same intervals between those hard wave breaks at night. Her rhythms were so peaceful. I had forgotten how well she moved with the water. The water puts grace in everyone, though, you glide, you float, you lose your limp . . .

But after fifteen minutes of up-and-downs, she was done, and Matt gave it up a few minutes later; then even Claire with her tank had had enough of it. Once they were accustomed to the turtles and the red of the coral they had seen all there was at this dive site. It would have been a monotonous day diving if we all had done it with tanks.

I surfaced again finally and Matt swam out to put me in a headlock and to tell me to get out, he was bored as socks. I gave him a kidney shot and heard him laughing up on the surface. I was down for another two and a half minutes. The sea turtles had gone in, and I must not have taken a deep inhale. Without the others, the waters now went cool and barren, the life suspended and still, sterile, the ocean lay open and unbearing. I was only weak. I wanted to surface, but the ocean wouldn't squeeze me from it. I only rose slowly through the water.

I surfaced and gasped.

twenty-two. *the elkhorn*

Back on the boat, Lawrence was sleeping or faking it, sitting stuffed into a metal chair next to Rainer's boy by the wheel. The divemaster still sat alone on the bow, now smiling to himself. Claire was watching me get out of snorkel and fins.

Rainer's boy took us back in and I sat with Claire astern again. The sun was humming in the wake. The others left us alone. She sat in a white bikini and wasn't topless this time without her husband. Her brown eyes were like a young girl's I once had seen watching balloons rise one morning in Leicester Square. I wasn't falling for her.

She had put her fins between her legs. Her legs were wet, tanned darkly in the sun. One fin had a slick on it.

"You have to watch the elkhorn," I said.

"It was a beautiful coral, so bright," she said. "You can not blink it away."

"I think you touched it," I said.

"I didn't," she said.

I took the fin from between her damp legs. She parted her knees when I lifted it and was trying to catch my eye.

"Coral slime," I said. "On your fin."

"It must have brushed accidentally."

"It'll burn for three days if it touches bare skin."

"I am embarrassed," she said.

"It's only an accident," I said.

"But it is like touching the living ocean walls. There was no drifting today, no reason for touching it."

She wasn't holding her bare finger now. I didn't ask about him. She had sent him away three weeks ago and still would be missing him.

"Still will you dive with me now?" she asked.

"Of course," I told her, "why not?"

Rainer's boy had the boat moving quickly. The wind was playing with her hair.

"You never look at me," she said. "I know why."

"I look at you."

"You do not really look at me," she said.

I looked at her but didn't hold her eye. She was resting her tongue in the corner of her mouth.

"Have you ever seen Leicester Square in the morning?" I said.

"No," she said. She unclasped a gold anklet, sliding it off her shin. "You are in love with her."

Jen and Matt lay together on a pad up by Lawrence's feet. She rested a hand on Matt's chest and he slept. Jen was blinking against the sunlight and I couldn't tell if she had been watching us. I couldn't see her blue eyes.

"You do love her," Claire said again.

"I already told you about that," I said.

"I told you," she said.

The boat bucked on a hidden terminal bar, sanding the wake, and Jen lay her head back down on Matt's chest, closed her eyes. Matt still was asleep. Behind them Lawrence was snoring, dreaming of disease.

"You will not meet me later?" Claire asked. She touched my chin. She guided my stare, finally, into her eyes, walks together in twilight and late at night through the dead palms on the beach,

and a false sun, perhaps, a bonfire licking at the night, and why?
For one Summer only. Surely, only for the rest of one Summer.

"Okay," I said.

The sea was open violet and flat, and we were the only boat
out. The casuarinas ashore were waving at us. We did not touch.

A Cure *for Gravity*

We were discussing again the question of the Past, in our cozy little ward upstairs. Of particular interest was the loss of our memories. The sun had shifted and recast the window sills and threw new spectrum and shadow across our surplus steel beds. Dry flurries of heat ebbed and waned. Down on the canyon rim, rattling in the afternoon gales, a rusted sign declared us and our hospital *Property of Traflow Base, USAF.* Again and again, we chronicled our earliest memories—our arrivals here—and the events of the days passing since. The development of moon phases, sunrises and sunsets, turning shade on faultlines down on the valley floor, even, again, recollections of the day it had rained. We were pretty sure the universe was still in order. Except, that is, for the four of us. We found ourselves trapped, as usual, between our portable i.v.s and an ether of ozone, between our ever-changing bandages and the ability to dream—without quite remembering—about the touch of water in clouded swimming pools, the scent of a freshly cut yard, and the brave sight of rain gutters hanging off their bolts, barely alive, waiting for us to fix them. The pastel walls here did nothing to improve the mood. Our frustrations mounting, we decided to venture out into the sunlight, to wait for the F-14s to come in crashing again, and to water our new patch of grass.

Down a shadowed staircase, a shattered step, a worn landing, through the tall oak doors always left ajar, shy as rabbits we nose our way out into the periphery and heat. With our portable i.v.s squeaking in the soil, gingerly we step down the slope to the edge of Red Canyon, a thousand-foot drop which might as well measure infinity.

Despite our efforts to save our little project, our grass is crinkling in the sun. It is a mix-Kentucky fescue. Hearty enough, we once thought. The blades no longer hold moisture, and that wonderful boundary in the soil, that distinction between barren death and our new green life, is beginning to blur. We water the tiny square of lawn with our eyes in blue yonder, searching for those pieces of silver which fall into the valley below. The cool spray from the hoses tickles our arms. Two miles off, nested down between the valley walls, Air Force barracks like mirrors reflect falling sun and hide emergency crews who stand on alert—with hoses in hand, too—and whose business is like ants.

"Government planning," says Grif, tossing his greasy cap over the edge. The cap hovers for a moment in the updraft, then flutters back to him. "An Air Force base on the floor of a valley."

"Beautiful day for a show, huh, Captain?" says Corcran, struggling over on a casted leg. Scorpions dance inside his eyes.

"Yes," I agree, though still uncomfortable with my ceded Captainhood. They say, though, this is how all rank is achieved.

"Filings of tin on a blue sheet of glass," says Grif.

"Yes, here comes one," says Asiz, absentmindedly digging a trough in the dirt with his stream of water. The first day we planted he nearly washed away all the seed, diamonds over the edge.

"Asiz," I say, "the grass."

"Sorry, Captain," Asiz says, feeling for the cowlick he can never keep down.

"Asiz is a spy," says Corcran.

"Asiz is a spy," mumbles Grif.

"I am only Egyptian," Asiz pleads.

"Men," I say, "can we come up with something newer?" Although Asiz does have brown wobbly eyes which never make contact.

"Yeah, this guy has no chance," Corcran says, "a ruin in the making."

We watch the drowsy jet trying to steady itself on blue sky without bearings, before that dip down into the canyon where the pilot then must level off and swerve to miss jutting rock for a mile and a half. Often they pass at eye level, and when they do we have learned that this means they are coming in too high and too fast for proper descent.

"Everybody wave," says Corcran, and we do as the jet passes in a rush of wind and roar. We imagine a turning pilot's helmet wondering who we are.

"He'll blend right in with the canyon," says Grif, as the red engines turn to dots.

"Look for a chute," says Asiz, "a twisting, delicate chute."

"Asiz is a pirate," says Corcran, and then the plane has fallen into another of those noiseless plumes before the distant line of asphalt.

"Government planning," says Grif.

"They rarely eject," says Asiz. "They fly in like heroes."

"Not even a goddamn echo," says Corcran. "How humiliating."

By bleary tributaries on crinkled parchment, our memories folded and unfolded, by this map you could have found us. Locate the darkest jagged line, the rapids running dry in the valley below (now not even a rivulet to recall old cutting force); trace terrain a thousand feet by scale to your right, up the canyon wall; locate the two-lane road hugging the edge. This is Sonic Highway, named for the booms the jets tear in the sky. Trails of mist, a white sandstone hospital perched above the canyon lip, here you would have found us, watering, muddying our hands in repair of grass follicles, nursing along our little patch of grass.

Mornings down in Red Canyon, sun lights up incomprehensible history, layers of sediment stacked up the gorge, black Vishnu Schist and Zoroaster Granite below, next Supai Sandstone stained with iron, then Hermit Shale and infections of lichen; the dawn of man doesn't appear until ten-thirty when the highest layers begin to shine red. From fossils to distant specks of white brittlebush in four and a half hours.

Perhaps we should venture down into the shaded, moist valley, down to all the lavender datura with their spiral petals, to the paradises and hells of hidden ecology. They say Nabokov discovered his Neonympha on an expired river's bed. But from here there exists no safe way to descend; the drop is fast and serrated, with rocky spurs and relics of ancient snowmelt.

Inside, blinking, the walls stay peach and we wait in our beds between windows which hang like portraits of blue sky. We wait for the Doctors, and for the Candy Man who provides cups full of pills we are encouraged to swallow. Our identities so young, we work with what we have.

"How are we today, men?"

"Not so good, Captain," says Asiz.

"Asiz is a bandit," says Corcran, flashing his scorpions again. Corcran calls his casted leg "Rebecca" and his good one "Susan." Susan never hurts and Rebecca always does.

"Grif?" I ask.

"I have a numb lip, sweaty balls, and I follow the Red Sox."

"I'm sorry, Grif. Nothing to do about that last one."

"Nothing to do about any of them," says Grif, spitting a sunflower seed into an empty bedpan. He turns in his bed to put his feet at his pillow and his head at the pan. He has been here longest.

"That crap about dry heat being more bearable is crap," Corcran says, bouncing Rebecca on his mattress, "especially when you're sharing a ward with a bandit."

"Why do you say this?" says Asiz. "You are making me weak."

"Asiz is a bandit," says Grif.

"I'm getting weaker with this talk," says Asiz, feeling for his cowlick again.

"What about you, Captain?" Corcran asks.

"I have a sore neck."

"I think I hear another jet," says Asiz.

"Bandit," whispers Corcran.

A distant rumble, and "Captain," Grif now says, "I think you should know. I've been keeping a tally of how much these planes crashing is costing the taxpayer."

The breeze rushes through, cracking tremors, another pilot flying in his thunder, shaking our beds. We can taste his exhaust.

"These jets are no good for my condition," Asiz cries, as the boom turns to scream. "Look for a chute. A billowing, majestic chute."

We love to watch them float gently down through the eras of canyon rock, Permian, Devonian, Cambrian, Pre-Cambrian, down they float until the canyon floor, where they dust themselves off and stand up solidly in the past, instead of just obliterating themselves against the Pleistocene Epoch. It's been days since a chute.

"That figure," Grif says to fill a new silence, "is one followed by twenty-seven zeros billion trillion dollars."

Here, they cure almost anything. Dry mouth, gout, in-grown nails, and measles. Hamstrings unluckily lacerated, infections of strep, insomnia, heartburn, fractured femurs from starts given by the plaid sidewinders outside. They treat hepatitis, too—only B so far, though they say we might also expect A—as well as red face, blue face, black lung, and pink eye. Influenza, e-bola, e-cola, and the plague (bubonic, primarily, though they anticipate a comeback of pneumonic), even smallpox, scurvy, and, of course, cardiac arrest. Also, gingivitis, laryngitis, mad cow's disease, bad breath. They say all of the above have a common cause—perhaps are symptoms of stress. So many to choose. Our aches and pains, once minor, since have evolved and carried us in and out of infirm states.

The Doctors, who always speak another language, approach our beds in threes to mock the Wise Men. Though our own origins are a secret, we have managed to discover that we are foreigners here. Each doctor wears a silver bowl on his forehead centered within which is a sharp white light which never burns out. Grif, in his expertise, provides us with translations.

"We are seeing fabulous reconstruction of the metatarsal," they tell Corcran.

"Grif?" asks Corcran.

"They say the bone is healing very well in your Rebecca."

"You have a minor C6-7 trauma," the Doctors tell me.

"Captain, they say you have a very sore neck."

"A series of myocardial infarctions and aortic abnormalities has allowed a new persuasion of staphylococcus to register in the left ventricle antipathetic to your immuno system," they tell Asiz, backing away in unison and leaving.

"Oh, I cannot take this," says Asiz. "Griffen, what are they saying to me?"

"Your heart's broken, Asiz. They say you're a goner."

"Asiz is a goner," says Corcran. "Ha-ha."

"A goner? That's it?" asks Asiz.

"And a Nazi," says Grif.

"Oh, I am so weak," says Asiz. "I am Egyptian only." He holds his ring finger which has swollen every day since the Doctors took our wedding rings away so we wouldn't accidentally swallow them in our sleep.

"Say something in Egyptian then," Corcran says. "Prove it."

"Something in Egyptian," Asiz says in Egyptian, which they say is a delicate language, despite its harsh sound.

"That's not very nice," Corcran says.

"What?" says Asiz.

"You just told him the Red Sox blow."

"I did nothing," says Asiz.

"Did you?" Grif asks, sitting up. "You slimy Saudi son of a bitch."

"Egypt," says Asiz. "Not Saudi."

"I know Egyptian," says Corcran. "And you said the Red Sox blow."

"I did nothing."

"I knew you were a Nazi," says Corcran.

"Asiz is a Nazi," mumbles Grif.

"Now I am too tired," says Asiz.

"Nazis get tired," Corcran says. "And they have bad hearts, like you."

"Corcran, now you must make up your mind," says Asiz. "Am I a bandit, a pirate, or a Nazi?"

"You're a spy," says Corcran.

"I thought so," says Grif.

On days when the fog pours over the canyon's edge and the valley is draped under a silk sheet and the pink fishhook cacti flowers close early for false night, the Candy Man is never on time. The Candy Man is a hairy-armed ape of a man crammed into a nurse's white skirt and white blouse. "Now, Asiz, be a good Asiz and take your candy," he says in a voice like a lullaby. The candy smells like sulfur and tastes like sugar. I always spit out the pills or flick them onto the cold brick floor without reprisal, though they say that in the end the only one to be hurt by my actions will be me.

"Asiz," the Candy Man says again, leaning like Pisa Tower over Asiz's bed, "you simply must take your candy."

"I say no to candy today," says Asiz. He wipes his forehead and examines the sweat on his fingertips.

"Griffen?" asks the Candy Man.

"Hello, gorgeous. Yes, please."

"And how about you, Corkie?"

"I do the opposite of Asiz."

"I know better than to ask the Captain," says the Candy Man, winking at me. "Tu-tu-lu, boys," he sings on his way out.

"If I could remember anything," Grif says, after the Candy Man has gone, "I'm sure that guy would remind me of my first wife."

"Mine, too," says Corcran, "if I could remember."

We know that the Candy Man dresses only for effect, that he is really only a hospital administrator or some high government official who desperately must conceal his true identity and does so in a veil of white skirts and hairy arms, which I believe they refer to as dramatic prerogative. He stokes our imaginations. He helps us to believe that we were brought here by government plot, that we are a part of some terrific government experiment, and that we are prisoners, though not prisoners, because they have made it explicitly clear that we may leave (though they never encourage us to leave before our "sentences" expire). We know that along with the base down in the valley, the government owns the whole canyon, the miles of chain-link land around the mouth, even the solitary, wandering bighorn rams. And so, too, the pills the Candy Man feeds us, and so, too, our i.v.s. And so, too, our questions. Some nights the government owns everything.

Though it is only our paranoia, it still is quite comforting to create explanations for having memories only a few weeks old, for having been lifted off the timeline. Thus our attempts to find a government connection. Some nights the conspiracy involves the Great Wall and Amelia Earhart, some nights Greta Garbo and the *Queen Elizabeth II*. Some nights the whole situation is the fault of our new grass, until I remind the men that we planted it ourselves, after we came here, and so it couldn't have been that.

"Yes," says Grif, gazing out the open windows to stars and heat lightning, "but if time were moving backward . . ."

"Grif—"

"Sorry, Captain. Speculating is all."

"I think it's an inside job," says Corcran, sweating through his shirt. "And I notice Asiz has been very quiet."

"Very good, Corcran," says Asiz, "it only took you eight seconds of a conversation before you accused me of something."

"Well, if Grif is right about time moving backward I was only replying to your rebuttal. So you started it."

You see how we get.

Often we stare through the windows south down the canyon, pink and open like an oyster beyond Traflow's shining barracks, out through strokes of shadow and sun to Lava Run, black in the day, thirteen million years old, and to Platinum Plateau mediating between ground and sky. It is the same view as in an old etching which is bolted to our ceiling, rendered, according to caption, by one of "F. W. Egloffstein's survey team." The caption also says it is "a picture of grandeur so misconstrued it remains today unidentified with known landscape." Grif says F. W. Egloffstein's wife left him for a high school boy.

Eventually orderlies with mustaches, attitudes, and dirty hands bring in a late lunch on wide silver trays. They feed us roast fake turkey with an original aroma, and a nut resembling a macadamia, which they say is not really a nut at all and should be classified as a fruit. We are silent until the orderlies leave. Once one of the big ones smacked Asiz for asking for a fork instead of a spork. The roast fake turkey is made of turkey stuffs and is sculpted by some artist to look authentic, but he can never quite get the drumsticks to match.

"I believe this turkey is suspect," whispers Asiz.

"Shit with your eyes closed," says Grif.

They say that a century ago Havasupai tribesmen once tracked game down in the canyon. We swallow our lunch and imagine sunlit ghosts dancing down along the amorous rim, desperately haunting their old geography.

Another night. The men are talking upstairs, and I sit with my i.v. on the steps outside under the window, counting stars to two hundred thousand something something and four, finally feeling drier with a few days off the candy. I shudder in a cold exhale up off the valley. The canyon walls are inflamed under moonlight, though the moon hasn't yet risen into view. Something something and five. . . . They say there is a place along the Nile where the heavens are a brain, and the Milky Way is the hazy divider between hemispheres of the mind. They say.

"And the pyramids are a hoax," Grif's voice is drifting through the open window above.

"Built by aliens," says Corcran.

"They were built by Egyptians!" cries Asiz.

"Never," says Grif. "If the Captain were here he'd tell you."

"You think it must be aliens because no dark skin person could do it," says Asiz.

"That's damn right," says Grif.

"Well, I have news, dark skin people have indeed built the greatest monument to man ever."

"It was aliens," says Corcran. "Giant cows. From Moopiter, to be specific."

"Don't take it personal, Asiz," Grif says, "the Gooks couldn't have built it either."

"You are racist," says Asiz.

"Everybody's racist," says Grif.

"I suppose you think you skinny-shouldered whites could build a pyramid?" Asiz says.

"White guys? Shit, no," says Grif. "That's the best one yet. White guys build runways at the bottom of canyons."

There is our grass, little fragile tufts, quivering down in the wind. Planted by us one morning, red sand and rock before, add seed, now blades, soon to be something else—taller grass or dead—then something else again, new dust. I try shaking the government interference out of my head. I know I haven't always been like this. I see the moonrise and fireflies. Across the other side of the valley, I see a shimmering line tracing the canyon edge. It is the north end of Sonic Highway, that road always camouflaged in daylight by the shadows of terrain.

A new breeze. And snapshots. I see a car, frozen in speed in an afternoon past. The windows are open to sun and dust off the asphalt. From that speeding car's window, I see a view, creases of canyon, then a void of valley falling off an edge without guardrail. I see a solitary cactus, a sentry standing by the road in salute. To the east: a mile of sand to pale, fleshy hills. I see a story to connect my snapshots. I see her.

Perhaps this is the same as memory.

She and I were driving a jagged line, that edge along the canyon which proved the world was flat. It was just the two of us, and with the heat so mean we sat in our underwear. We were tired and sticking to the old leather seats. We smelled like smoke.

The radio was trapped between static and men talking about the future of something and a soprano glued seemingly forever to mid-octave. A baby's rattle rolled between us on the seat cushions and ticked with the sway of the car. We were on base property without permission again.

She was wearing one of her silver infinity earrings, those sideways figure eights, still left on from the night before "out with her friends." One of her earrings was missing. Despite our increasing speed, I kept the old car true to the bending road, and we were still holding hands.

She was hungover, so she was telling me about philosophy.

"When you deconstruct the mind," she says, putting her feet up on the dash, "you realize the intricacies of all its competing desires and messages. Lust and Love, for instance. It's really quite marvelous. Foucault questions whether there even will be any human beings in the future. I mean human beings as an organizing concept. Right now we see a person as a collection of all these competing voices and wants. What if someday we only identify the competing voices and wants and forget about calling the collection a human being?"

She squeezes my hand for emphasis. She pokes her toe at the windshield like a pointillist. "Then you're left with the worst kind of extinction," she says, squinting into the sun. "Not physical extinction, but worse. Conceptual extinction."

I wondered if she wanted me to ask about the ghost in the machine. Her neck, her hairline were wet. I asked how her headache was.

"I know what you're thinking," she says, dropping her hand from mine. "You're a predictable romantic. The ghost is gone if we deconstruct the mind. Anyway, God is dead by any name. The cure for humanity to survive conceptually is to remain a faithful collection of all our competing desires, and to acknowledge the competition within ourselves. I have to remain a sum of all my opposing parts, you know. Love and Lust, you know, together. Not one or the other. I have to live out all my contradictions."

She was fooling with a bracelet. The slender shape of her wrist . . .

"So what's happened," she says, "is that I've decided, simply, to begin acting on those minor needs that I haven't given time to before. Like last night. With Larry in his pool. For the sake of humanity—my own—and as a step ahead for everyone, too, really."

The highway ends. I had only asked where her missing earring was. I was swerving and skidding us on clay soil, catching a spinning glimpse of a sandstone building across the canyon. The rear axle finally came to rest a few feet from the drop. The two of us were breathless and so vulnerable in our underwear, our white thighs and stomachs ridiculously innocent. We were facing safely, at least, the soft hills eastward.

This is the same as memory. The surroundings fade as she drives back into evening sky without me. Alone I sit in our skids on the road, ashamed of the bloom of sentiment burning my neck, my face. My neck, really, is a whiplashed wreck. Heat lightning flickers a false autumn storm. Like flashbulbs.

More snapshots. A man with no face trimming an overgrown hedge. A lawnmower on its side, rusting in a downpour. A father's briefcase, open, papers flapping in a breeze.

A seared page in an old book, we turn over another morning. The Candy Man takes Asiz's chin in his giant hands. Asiz's forehead has been wrapped in gauze. "Asiz," says the Candy Man, "be a doll and swallow these today." This morning the Candy Man appears only to be a very big-boned woman with a hormonal imbalance.

"I feel the strength of ten migraines coming on," Asiz says.

"Darling, you simply must then take your medicine."

"No. And when you say 'darling' it has a very bad old ring in my head for some reason."

"Darling, the rest of them take these."

"I have noticed that the rest of them do not," says Asiz, squirming in his sheets. "Specifically for instance the Captain."

"Yes," the Candy Man says, wagging a finger at me. "I suppose the Captain was the original bad apple." Then he or she smiles and curtsies and leaves, again having won over only Corcran and Grif.

"How are we today, men?" I ask.

"It's my other leg," says Corcran. "Turns out, the whole time it was Susan."

"How about you, Grif?"

"I had a dream where at a Country Club all manner of women were accusing me of miscellaneous ineptitudes."

"I also had a dream," Corcran says, bouncing on his bed the cast they switched from leg to leg, wincing at the new pain Susan is giving him. "I dreamed Asiz was a thief."

"Asiz *is* a thief," Grif whispers, leaning back into a wet pillow.

"I am getting old with this talk," says Asiz.

"I can't find my blanket," shouts Corcran. "Asiz took it!"

"There's never any need for blankets," I say.

"Then Asiz took my imaginary blanket," Corcran says.

"Imagine a new one," I say.

"Asiz is imaginary," Grif mumbles.

"Ha-ha. Asiz is imaginary," Corcran says. "Hey, Grif, it's so hot, can the rest of us be imaginary today, too?"

"No philosophy," I say, even though we are harmless. Our madness this morning seems only a mirage, only a distraction from an embarrassing grief.

Moonlight pours through our windows. Corcran stirs.

"Captain," he says, "are you awake?"

"Yes."

"I am awake, too," says Asiz.

"We're all awake, dumb-ass," says Grif.

"Let's go outside for the midnight flights," Corcran says.

"We never go down this time of day," I say. The base is lit again tonight, a string of pinpricked bulbs and a runway bordered by green flares. A tiny city submerged in darkness.

"Who's going to notice?" asks Grif. "The Doctors are gone, that giant nurse, everybody."

"Come on, Captain," Corcran says. "Screw the time. Nobody ever sleeps anyway."

"I, too, am for viewing the heroes," says Asiz.

Sensing a mutiny, I agree to lead us from our beds. Down the moonlit stairwell, over silhouettes of broken lipstick cases, through the smells of roses never delivered, hand in hand we creep: a sore neck, a numb lip, a broken Susan or Rebecca, a hurting head and lousy heart. The doors downstairs, open for us again, are a rectangle of stars and moonlight. So out we go.

At the top of the slope, having left behind our i.v.s at my suggestion, we pause in the freedom of night sky and breeze. Our eyes water in the moonlight. The air smells like smoke, like piles of leaves we each might have once burned in our own backyards. They say that in an earlier era the base below once

operated accident-free, before the supersonics and their inability
to fly in at safe speeds. The scorpions have disappeared from Corcran's gaze.

"I would like to say to everyone that I have a revelation," says
Asiz. My heart kicks at the idea of someone else's head clearing a
little, too. I have been hoping for this, for a few days off the pills
to work a little magic for one of the others.

"I am a spy," Asiz says, smiling. His gauze headwrap shines.

"That's better," says Corcran, holding up an imaginary cup.
"Want some of my coffee?"

"I thought he'd never admit it," says Grif. "What a relief."

And then they turn to me, their eyes glistening not so playfully in the moonlight.

"Captain?" asks Corcran.

"Yes?"

"You're really a Captain, aren't you?"

"Okay."

"Well, now that is a great relief," says Corcran. "We can call
off the investigation."

"Yeah," Grif says. "To be honest, we had bitterly mismanaged
the inquiry anyway. Half the invisible men I put on the job
couldn't even read."

"It's no offense, Captain," Corcran says. "It's just that you
weren't taking the pills. Plus I have trust issues."

"We don't have to take the pills," I say. "They're sort of a temporary fix."

"We don't have to take the pills?" Grif asks, staring up at the
hospital walls, now luminous and white.

"No."

"Well. I'm still taking them," Grif says.

"Asiz," Corcran says, "how'd you like to spy for our team?"

"Yes," says Asiz, "very much."

"Welcome aboard," says Grif.

"Boy, we really are crazy," Corcran says.

"Yes," says Grif. "I agree completely."

But how can I tell them? There is drama in our madness, even sense of purpose, albeit somewhat misguided. But men with only broken hearts are laughingstocks.

"Two minutes until twelve," says Asiz, and stripe-tailed cacomistles scamper like prowlers in the sand.

"Grif," I say, "how much longer are you in for?"

"They say I have another ten months."

"Corc?"

"I have a year and a half left."

"I forget," Asiz says, holding his forehead. "I am looking forward to taking the pills again."

"How about you, Captain?" asks Grif, chewing on a new sunflower seed.

"I think I only have another few weeks."

"There must be some kind of formula for figuring out our sentences," Grif says.

I whisper that I think it's probably something like two months for every year you were in a relationship with her.

"What?" shouts Corcran.

"I believe the Captain is trying to jog our memories," Grif says.

"I decided I like mine the way it is," Corcran says.

"Yes," says Asiz. "She is much simpler this way."

Then we hear the old thunder, distant and steady.

"Captain," Corcran says, saluting, "will you do the honors?"

Slowly I lead us down the slope, the loose soil, the sliding footsteps, down to the chasm's lip. I should say more to the men, but there is peace in my cowardice. Anyway, they are comfortable here, at this hospital kept for men like us.

"Yes, we never go down at night. This is much better," says Asiz. "Look for a chute, a twirling, gossamer chute."

Our grass crackles under our feet. It stands like white hairs (brown, to be honest, in the true light of day). The cold drafts off the chasm tingle in our cheeks. We search for a moving star, await his big approach. Across the canyon, Sonic Highway glitters like old magic, and reminds me, once again, of her. Everyone is unhappy differently, she once told me. She was wrong about this. Here comes the roar.